"We are HUMAN!

Our brains, our sensuality are a mighty power that mocks the agony of the land with a force that only the universe can know. We must LIVE, live on. Now, now, NOW, hurry, while we can still know it, while we can still FEEL. It is ecstasy and pain. Pain! PAIN! The world is afire! The world is burning,

B-U-R-N-I-N-G!"

When the screaming girl at last lay still, calmed by the injection, the doctor spoke to Wesley Harmon. "This is a classic re-action, if we can apply that phrase to something so new. Every woman afflicted with these symptoms has had one of these in her possession." He swung the gem in mid-air, "This psychic pendant!"

GENETIC BOMB

Andrew J. Offutt
and
D. Bruce Berry

WARNER
PAPERBACK
LIBRARY

A Warner Communications Company

WARNER PAPERBACK LIBRARY EDITION
First Printing: August, 1975

Cover illustration by V. DiFate

Warner Paperback Library is a division of Warner Books, Inc.,
75 Rockefeller Plaza, New York, N.Y. 10019.

 A Warner Communications Company

Printed in the United States of America

·Not associated with Warner Press, Inc. of Anderson, Indiana

To Jodie and Leonida
neither of whom is a girl.

ONE...

Shrieking madness lurched across the airless waste, crying out to the stars that burned coldly, disdainfully: "No! Damn it *no*! I'm a MAN! It can't *happen*!"

The woman ran from her home, screaming with laughter, trailing a tangle of wild hair. Waving the dripping knife in her smeared fist, she screamed in pride that she had saved her children, saved them from the cataclysm——

——emerged from the smashed window, all laughing as they hurled bright jewels into the writhing, humid air. The policer saw them, drew his enforcer ... and hurled it through that portion of the window that remained unbroken. He plunged in even as it crashed and tinkled, and more precious stones and jewels for milady's roasting melting arms sparkled in the air as he emerged laughing to join the vandals——

——Burning winds surrounded them and his hands felt hot on this last night of terror. She gave him her lips, urged them on him, and when his mouth and body took command of hers she trembled more than the quaking land. Then they were sinking down, pressed tightly together: *Hurry! Hurry! On this final night of blazing madness we have only one last ch*——

"No! You can't DO IT!"

Sweating shrieking horror stumbled over cold desolation. "I can get out of this. I know I can make it ...

millions, millions, do you hear me, *millions*! But not THIS —not the end!"

Hurry, hurry! We have so little time and the doomstar is rising! Look, it's like a ball of blood on the—— The ground heaved beneath her. Stones pressed into her back in welcome pain/pleasure. Her lover whispered endearments into her ear with more urgency than ever before——

——came rushing down the street to plow into the great structure of steel and cement and plastic, spilling its dwellers out heaving windows as it buckled, flames gouting——

No, she screamed, shrieking to hear herself above the thundering, sundering world. And he was pressing in, in, wiping out the horror of final damnation. The end the end the end end end . . . They writhed, sweating, so great and good, spreading warmth into her in a mounting flame. Hotter than the burning sky and the tottering, flaming world and its boiling seas. Thrust! No more tomorrows! The world is burning, BURNING, B-U-R-N-I-N-G——

Shrieking madness staggered across knife-sharp rocks. "I'm a man! I'm a MAN!" Insane laughter bubbled from the shattered, boiling brain. Nightmare-propelled, it raced across the cold, dead stone without knowledge of the thing that was crawling inexorably up from the depths of its psyche.

"Looming above the horizon like some bloated obscenity, that rising star of death and madness. Clouds racing across the sky like terror on wings before the final storm of all eternity. The oceans rising to meet it, the flames of a tormented world erupting into the red burning air. Love, love, LOVE! Take me, while the ground thunders beneath our feet and heralds the final darkness without end

end end end

"He tears the cloak from me, springs the catches of my jerkin, and I am bared to the hot winds. The passion in me leaps forth to him as, frantically, I strive to drown the sounds of horror with

8

his mouth. This is all we have left! I want it so much, this last taste of the nectar of life! He presses against me, his hard body with the superb muscles, succor against the horror. I want it all, him, all all this wonder that I can hold within me.

"It will be the last, the last!

"Savagely, he grips me, crushes me tight to him. Hot ashes of burning cities sting our bodies as we sink to the crumbling, ripping pavement. A man rushes past with a dripping ax. A girl follows him, screaming and wailing, begging . . . for his ax in her brain, not his body in hers. Another scream, and I turn my head to see another writhing as I am, in this last and supreme human rite:

"The creation of life, a mocking taunt to the cataclysmic destruction of all life.

"Sweating groaning writhing death horror redness black *end*

"I urge him on with cries of desperation: *Hurry! Hurry! We have so little time left!* The ground quakes beneath us, as fearful as we.

"He is mine! We are man and woman, we refuse death, we defy it and the redness in the sky. Wonderfully hard and deep, with a power I never dreamed he possessed. A heat grows in me, hotter than the burning world around us, hotter than the sky raining ashes and sparks. Panting, sweating, I tell him with desperate urgency all the things I have never told him, all the things I have whispered a hundred, a thousand times before.

"We are HUMAN! Our brains, our sensuality are a mighty power that mocks the agony of the land with a force that only the universe can know. We must *live*, live on—I scream for the magic moment and the world screams around us. My voice is lost in hurricanes of wind-blown fire: *Now, now,* NOW, *hurry, while we can still know it, while we can still* FEEL! A thundering, hot river, and we have come together in a magnificent farewell to the stars. The beautiful stars, a skyful of pearls that has vanished, blotted out by the flaming sky that we used to watch, smiling, on cool and quiet nights when there was no urgency, only—

"I scream in ecstasy and pain. Pain! PAIN! The world is afire! The world *burns*! Death and horror, death and *transfiguration*!

"The world is burning, the world is burning, B-U-R-N-I-N-G!

The little gun made a thumpswish noise, jetting a sedative into the girl's arm. Her contorted face stared, mouth writhing, and relaxed. She sagged. She was wet, glistening with perspiration.

The doctor rose shakily to his feet, wiping the sweat from his own forehead. He sucked in a great breath, held it for a moment, and let it out slowly. Then he turned to look at the other man.

"Well, you've heard it. It was very real to her. Now you have an idea what we're up against." Seating himself behind his desk, he opened the reelwood box, took out a 'Pulco Gold and lit it as if it were his first. But the careful, deep-sucking way he inhaled told the other man that it was not. The doctor held the smoke for a long time before releasing it as carefully and slowly as he had his breath, a minute before. He looked up again.

"You have a *small* idea, I should have said, of what we're up against, Harmon."

Wesley Harmon nodded, taking a Java from his pack. He ignited the tip and joined the physician in a relaxing smoke. He smoked carelessly, like a man who need not worry about the price of the best emjay available. He stared thoughtfully at the unconscious girl, her babbling ended by the injection.

"I've never heard anything like that from her before. Never." He shook his head. "It sounded almost like a—a recording. Just not Nancee."

The doctor shrugged. His face was beginning to sag back into its normal hound-dog lines. "People's voices often change, in a state of shock." He nodded at the girl. "But they don't always behave like *that*, believe me. You might call this a classic reaction, if we can apply that phrase to something so new."

"You see it as a disease, Doctor Cawdil? You expect more of this . . . delusion?"

"Well, they describe the same thing," Cawdil said, frowning. His eyebrows were heavy and thick, ambushing pale eyes. "Some aspect of the same thing, anyhow: world destruction. And the erotic effect, nearly every time. It seems to be what they want to be doing as they . . . go out. Perhaps if the end of the world ever arrives, that's what we'll all be doing. One last ecstat."

Harmon looked sidewise at him. "Couldn't it be suppressed desires?"

"You don't seem to be the sort of man who would leave his girls repressed," the doctor said, lifting an eyebrow, and Wes returned his smile. "Besides, it isn't easy for anyone to have repressions in this world of ours, Harmon. The Freewill laws give us every right. We—either sex— can indulge in any libidinous fantasy to our heart's content." He nodded at the girl. "So can she. And the real thing is constantly available to us. Certainly you know that."

Leaving his cigaret, he rose and bent over the girl to unfasten her necklace. He flourished it, swinging the pendant so that it glittered and seemed to leave a fiery wake in the air.

"I would have taken this off her first thing, but you wanted to see the whole effect."

"What makes you so certain that's what's causing it?" Harmon reached for the necklace.

Doctor Cawdil drew the piece of jewelry back, out of the other man's reach. "Better not touch it." He smiled, or rather his mouth did. "Please don't think I'm giving credence to . . . sorcery. It just happens, Harmon, that every woman afflicted with these symptoms has had one of these in her possession."

He swung the gem again, as though it were a psychic pendant, staring at it. "A Star Pearl." He sighed, then looked up from the precious bauble.

"Your last girl had one, but you didn't get there in time to see it. It's in the Guild vaults with the others— quite a few of them. They're still running laboratory tests

11

on the things. A private lab, of course. The government is as usual sitting back picking its collective nose. They've appointed a Study Commission, and they've added the Star Pearl to the list of illegal imports."

Harmon nodded. "But they won't do anything else unless there's an interplanetary complaint, yeah. What are the chances of that?"

Doctor Cawdil returned to his desk, retrieved the 'Pulco Gold butt, and sucked one last time. Then he dropped it through the center of the ashtray into the little well below. He shook his head.

"Minimal. Practically nil. Evidently the things are showing up only here on Earth, not on the other two planets. And so far, distribution per population percentage doesn't 'warrant any great alarm,' as the official handout put it. Too, the fact that the pearls aren't *killing* anyone puts them in the category of an irritating narcotic, total effect and means unknown." He sighed. "We haven't proved even that, empirically."

"Cause-effect."

"Yes, but we haven't *proved* that. *Is* there a . . . a 'Star Pearl Syndrome'?" Again he swung the necklace gently, manipulating the sparkling stone. "It—looks almost alive, doesn't it?"

Wes puffed his cigaret for the last time, squinting through the pallid smoke at the gem. He shrugged. "Any stone does, with the light on it."

"You'll change your mind in a minute," Cawdil said, dropping the necklace into his pocket with a tight chuckle. He repacked his little medicase and snapped it shut before turning to the nurse, ignored and immobile across the room, staring at the girl who had seen doomsday.

"If she shows any signs of arousing, give her another two cc's of Psychotran. A psychiatrist will be here in the morning, to prepare her for recon." He narrowed his eyes. "You all right, Rick?"

The nurse nodded. "I'm all right. Just wondering what she saw—and worrying a little. Do you have to carry that thing around in your pocket?'

12

"Not for long, you can be sure of that! Good night, Rick."

"Good night, Doctor," the nurse said, and nodded at Wes.

Doctor Cawdil led the way out into the darkened hall. He was drawing the necklace from his pocket as the door slurped shut behind them.

"Look now, Harmon, in the dark."

Wes looked. The jewel was *glowing*, with a faint light that seemed to pulse, like a heartbeat. A finger sheathed in ice drew a line up his spine.

As . . .

      as he . . .

           almost grasped the . . .

                the meaning of the gem? But he quickly readjusted his psychological pattern

           and laughed nervously. "First time I've ever seen a phosphorescent trick like that. No wonder they're popular. Neat trick."

"Isn't it, though." The physician thrust the necklace back into his pocket. "The ladies love it, even if it does drive them fobby." He shook his head, then shrugged. "Maybe it's the pulsations that do it, but we can't prove it. Self-hypnosis, maybe." He waved a hand at the wall, and light glowed in the hallway.

"I'd like to know more about these things," Wes said.

"Ha! So would the rest of us! But we don't even know where they come from. Well—let's go down and tell Bigcred our story."

Doctor Cawdil turned and walked down the hall. Following, Wes reached up a hand to—

tucked the covers around the sleeping j-girl and picked a piece of lint from his nurse's uniform and brushed the cloth smooth, admiring the girl's bosom

and crept cautiously through the shadows of the shrubbery toward the mansion, thumbing off the safety of his needler

—shift the weight of the old-fashioned pistol in the holster under his jac. He followed the doctor, frowning,

13

watching his bustling physician's stride, his white klamys flapping about his legs. Wesley Harmon's reputation depended on his ability to guarantee employment and safety for the girls he represented. Ordinarily, that was no problem. Gifts the girls received from their clients were usually quite harmless, nearly always personally decorative, and often expensive. But this was a different matter, a different gift, and a problem, a different sort of problem for a man whose emphatically good living derived from emphatically attractive young women.

Nancee was one of his finest practitioners, undisputed mistress of the more refined sensual arts. It was one hell of a shock for her to have experienced. He knew that; she was the second of his girls to go through it. The situation was becoming more than alarming. He was concerned, and he knew humping well he was justifiably concerned. Was someone plotting to destroy his business, or to drive him out of his mind?

Doctor Cawdil led the way down the wide descalator to the first floor and walked beside Wes across the richly furnished foyer. The paneled door looked too fine for reelwood. Wes checked; it was. He noted with more than casual interest that it was genuine oak and not a plastic substitute. Oak door and Star Pearls to j-girls! A client worth having—if the man just had a little sense.

The door swung in when the doctor rapped discreetly. More ostentation: a human butler glanced at them with monumental disinterest, then opened the door wider for their entry. She stepped back out of the way, though, when Wes showed no sign of angling.

Across the carpeted floor two men sat at an ornate desk—wood again, the real thing. Bigcred indeed! They were bent, serious-faced, over a disarray of papers and visispools.

The mustached man looked up and ran a hand through his hair; thick locks streaked with gray flopped loosely through his fingers, just as if they were the real item. His hand left it to shift to the more serious business of toying with the tip of his mustache, curling it. He rose.

"Come in, citizens."

14

They did, Wes watching the butler's departure through another door with appreciation. Her black cover-all looked as though it had been sprayed on in the dark; the spray had barely misted her in a few places.

Taking a seat in a leather-upholstered chair, Wes reached for another cigaret. The fact that one of the men was puffing on a troque, but that there was neither smoke nor smell in the room told Harmon of a fine filtration/conditioning system in operation. They would not recognize his illegal cigarets for what they were: real tobacco. He crossed his legs, gazing at the two men, tapping the cigaret on his nail. When he spoke, it was both quietly and coolly.

"She will survive, Fallman. Now I must seriously object—"

The other man interrupted him with a nod and a quick jerk of his hand. "I know, Harmon. My lawyer has been bawling shit out of me for it." He indicated his companion with a nod. "Blayr," he said, and Blayr nodded in silent greeting as Fallman leaned back in his chair. He spoke directly to Wes.

"I'm terribly upset about this myself, believe me. Nancee is a topnotch jay. She's always given me the greatest stisfaction. I'm more than fond of her. That's why I gave her the present, for godsake; I felt she deserved the finest money could buy. The most expensive gem was a Star Pearl."

"You know it's illegal to import those things," Doctor Cawdil said, sitting in a chair identical to Harmon's, a couple of feet away. The room was flagrantly spacious. So were the chairs.

"Of course, of course," Fallman said impatiently. "But it is *not* illegal to own one. I must admit I don't know how it reached Earth. I don't bother with such matters.. When I want something, I simply say so." He waved a hand. "Whatever it is, I can afford it."

"Good," Wes said, talking through expelled smoke. "Because that girl is going to receive the finest reconditioning your money can buy. I suppose you've made

15

arrangements for a settlement." It was only partly a question.

Fallman shoved a paper across the desk. "Yes."

When Wes made no move, Blayr said, "This authorizes you to bill my client for any expenses incurred in the girl's recovery and rehabilitation. Of course, that also includes compensation for your losses and the expenses you suffer from loss of her services."

"That," Wes said, "will be considerable. A girl of Nancee's specialized talents is an absolute necessity to a well-run procurement service. She was solidly booked for the next two months."

Fallman looked down. Without hurrying, Wes rose and picked up the document. It was already plastisealed, he noted, with Fallman's signature and stamped number and credfac. *Confident*, he thought, but as his eyes ran down the page he saw why: the agreement was just as the attorney had said. He could actually profit, if he wished. Good! He would, and he'd surprise Nancee with the windfall.

He folded the document and slipped it into a pocket. Plucking at the little ornament on the left lapel of his jac, he drew it up on its slender wire to his mouth. "Reminder: sign and seal agreement with Fallman and return him a fac." He released the microphone, which was reeled back to his lapel.

"Now, about the Star Pearls," he said, sitting down. "This is the second of my girls to receive one, and to have been . . . mentally affected. Jewelry's a magnet for any woman, and certainly I can't prevent mine from accepting jewels as gifts. That would be a violation of Freewill, for starts. But . . . we've got to take some steps to locate the source of these things."

Fallman raised an eyebrow. "We?"

"Well," Wes smiled, "I'm sure this little agreement is intended solely as compensation. Not as a persuader to me not to mention that my girl was given an illegally imported item, surely. Since I'm sure you've learned enough from this experience not to order another one, I'll say I don't intend to file a report. And Nancee won't, either,

I'll vouch for that." He leaned back in the big chair. "On the other hand, it puts me in a fine position to ask a man who can—as you said—afford anything, to help us track down these things. It might be expensive. They've cost me cred already. And, if we need more than a vutting good selfish reason: they're a menace to Earth."

"Are you intimating blackmail, Harmon?"

Wes glanced at the attorney, only that. "I didn't hear you."

"Relax," Fallman muttered in Blayr's direction. He pulled at his mustache. "What can we do to locate the source, Harmon? With all due respect to your profession, the embodiment of Freewill, you are after all not a member of GunTek or anything similar."

Wes examined the tip of his cigaret and managed, without effort, a smug smile.

"You're thinking of the ancient practitioners of my profession, Fallman. We're a solidly organized guild, and we're perfectly capable of making things extremely unpleasant for . . . for instance," he said, looking up into the man's eyes, "those who don't conform to the laws and our rules of operation. Frankly, we're prepared to . . . eliminate those responsible for distribution of these damned outerspace rocks." He smiled again, switching his gaze to Blayr. "It's a simple matter of being practical."

"I'm aware of both the legal powers and the . . . ah . . . potency of your guild, Harmon," the attorney said without the shade of a smile. "But—wouldn't it be better to leave it to the police?"

Wes shook his head in unequivocal disagreement. "You know better than that. The police are tied to and by Freewill. The girls accepted the gems of their own free wills, and that absolves the distributor of any legal responsibility—"

"—including my client—"

"—including your client, so that he's responsible *only* for aiding and abetting smugglers." Wes paused to be certain that one sank home. "All they could be tried for is violation of import laws. A little thought will show you most of the legal tangles involved." He recrossed his legs.

"But I didn't get that urgent call to come here for a legal seminar, which I'm sure neither of us needs." He returned his attention to the rich man. "Where'd you get your Star Pearl, Fallman?"

Fallman glanced at the doctor. "Do you have it?"

"Yes. And I'm keeping it. Long enough to turn it over to the Guild Directorate, that is. Not all your cred could buy it back."

Fallman snorted. "I wouldn't take it back at gunpoint! All right. The entire transaction took place anonymously, and through a man acting as agent for me. I simply dropped the word into the jewelry market that I was willing to buy one." He tapped the communicator on his desk. "I received a call very quickly. View-blanked and voice-rigged; professionals! We reached an agreement. The Pearl was delivered to my agent, who handed over the cred—in cash. I then had the stone mounted, and by a very reputable firm." He shrugged. "It's standard practice, all of it. There's no other way of getting them."

Wesley sighed. "Yeah. Understandable, considering the legal blocks. No sense checking back with your agent or trying to I.D. the call. Everything will be covered up."

He stood. "A guild rep will arrive in the morning to have Nancee transferred to a private hospital with full medical facilities." He moved to the desk and bent forward to grasp Fallman's hand. The other man rose quickly.

"Don't let this fob you overmuch," Wes said. He had the agreement in his pocket; the man was a wealthy client. "You won't be blacklisted for this, and I'll see that no one knows about the Pearl. The funds I'm going to steal out of our agreement will make Nancee happy."

Fallman started to frown, then smiled. He squeezed Harmon's hand. "I understand. You're an indecorously direct man, Harmon, and I'm delighted. Thank you—very much. And believe me, I'm terribly upset about Nancee, and that you were inconvenienced."

Wes gazed at him a moment, then turned to the doctor. "Are you going back to town?"

"Not right away, thanks. I think I'll stay an hour or so to be sure the girl is all right."

"Right. Good night." Wes paused at the door. "I'm really in love with this door, Fallman," he said, grinning, and he stepped through and closed it behind him.

In the front hallway, he paused to survey his features in the huge holomirror. With one finger he scratched the tip of his nose—

waiting impatiently outside the mansion in the deep shadows cast by the shrubbery, gun ready in a hand that was sweaty in its glove

—narrowing his eyes at his reflection. Harmon got rid of his cigaret in the sucker on the little hall table—not wood—and turned to examine the front door. He glanced up at the light, cocked his head, and shrugged. Why bother to turn it off? With a tight, grim smile he reached for the latch. His big hand swung the door open with ease, and he stepped quickly outside, every one of his senses as alert as any of the few wild animals left on Earth.

The man outside began shooting at once.

TWO...

The needles rapped out a little tattoo as they impacted the door behind Wes. He was already moving to one side, away from the light. His hand blurred into his jacket and reappeared full of the bulk of the unlikely gun he favored: an old-fashioned .45-caliber revolver. The big gun bucked savagely, noisily hurling leaden pellets into the darkness.

A shadow detached itself from that of the shrubs, lurching upright onto the spacious lawn. Needles spewed wildly from the muzzle of its gun in a desperate attempt to find the man behind the flaming pistol. But as the glittering hell poured from the man's little gun, Harmon's bullets tore through clothing and flesh. The assassin jerked back at the impact, reeling, rivering out his life.

An engine suddenly raced. Wes looked up to see the little car's lights and its bulk against the sky as it sped away. The driver was abandoning his comrade without even attempting to complete their task. Wes sighted, then sighed and lowered his gun. He trotted across the lawn to the man he'd shot, ready to fire again if necessary.

It wasn't.

Before going through the man's clothing, Wes ejected the cartridge casings and inserted new ones. The failed assassin carried no bag, and his pockets were empty. Wes wiped the blood back on the clothing of the dead man, rising as the other men came boiling out of the house.

Fallman reached him first, and Wes had time to wonder how often an unconditionally wealthy man went in for recon.

"What happened out here? What was all that—who's this?"

"A dead man," Wes told him. "No I.D. I'd say he's from GunTek."

"*Gun*—a reputable protection and technical service company? They wouldn't do anything like this, surely."

Wes looked at him. "Like what?"

"Like try to kill you," Fallman's attorney said, panting a little. "It's obvious, Harmon. The door's ruined, full of needles. But what was all the *noise*?"

"I don't like needlers. I use an old-fashioned gun. It blows holes in people, and he's more ruined than that door is. I'd hoped this sort of weapon would scare them off, but it isn't working."

"Hm?"

"This is the third time this month I've been shot at." Wes shook his head at Fallman, ignoring his and Blayr's shock at his choice of weapon. "You must lead a mighty protected life. Punch this into your tapes. GunTek sells anything it can get away with, the same as anyone else, and that includes killers." He glanced down. "Or would-be killers. You're going to have a lot of brown grass in the morning, Fallman."

The doctor rose from his examination of the corpse. "You use one hell of a vicious weapon, Harmon! Lord, what a hole! But surely you aren't unhurt."

"Not a scratch."

Doctor Cawdil frowned in disbelief. "If you say so— but why would someone be shooting at you?"

"And why," Blayr added, "haven't you reported it to the Guild? The other attempts, I mean?"

Wes shrugged. "Their needles aren't any harder than my bullets, and I think my aim must be better. They haven't been able to hit me yet."

Cawdil was looking about for something to wipe his his bloody hand on. Fallman and Blayr edged away from him, staring at the smears, then at Harmon. They kept

21

their distance from him, too. Violence was bad enough—but no one used such ghastly weapons any more.

The doctor was still frowning. "That doesn't sound like GunTek. I never heard of them missing—certainly not when they fired first. You sure you're untouched?"

Wes ignored the question. "Got any better ideas?"

"What?"

"If not GunTek, who?"

"Oh." The doctor shook his head. "No," he conceded, "none that wouldn't make this even more complicated."

"I think we'd better call the police," Blayr said.

"All right, counsellor, you've said it," Wes grinned. "Now advise your client properly. The police would just wonder why we wasted their time on a killed killer. What could they do that I haven't already done?"

"They could investigate, Harmon. Find out *why*."

"Bullsheet. That would only cause us trouble. Someone tried to kill me, in your yard, Fallman, and I one-upped him. Why don't you just get rid of the meat?" He jerked a thumb at the body.

Fallman nodded, glancing around at his silent guards. Two had come running up; another was examining the front door.

"Take care of this, Schwartz."

The guard nodded. "Yessir."

"Citizens," Wes said, "at the risk of repeating myself: good night."

"Harmon . . . yes. Good night."

"Be careful," Doctor Cawdil said.

"You be careful, Doctor," Wes called back. "You've got that vutting thing in your pocket, not me."

A few minutes later, locked into the traffic beam and settling back to let his car take him in, Wes smiled in satisfaction. He nodded to the admiring passersby who stared at his obviously expensive car as it whished past as the 2000-meter level.

He wasn't a four-bit schlock procurer, he was a licensed and successful one, and he was careful to put up the proper show. Quality is respected in all circles, and Show; and respect means a finer class of customers—men like

Fallman. The show was valuable both to the firm and to the girls who depended on Wesley Harmon

The towers of the metropolis were rapidly rising before him. Gleaming spears rising toward the night sky, glittering with that luminosity that turned concrete into a thing of beauty after the fall of shadows. The buildings of compacted garbage, too, possessed beauty, day and night. Harmon's hand dropped to the controls, automatically canceling the autopilot. He swung down through suburban towers to bring the machine to rest atop one of the shorter buildings. Turning it over to the attendant, Wes took the elevator down to the twentieth floor.

He felt comfortable now, relaxed, with his heels moving over the carpeted corridor. This floor was his, on long-term lease. It contained his offices/living suite, a room for his accountant and another for the guard-bouncer, and private apts for the girls. He was, after all, subject to heavy federal fine if he failed to provide satisfactory quarters and care for his heifers.

The fact was of no concern to him. He loved them all, and loved their loving, and was delighted to provide the best of surroundings.

He stopped before his door, cocking his head to gaze with some pride at its legend.

WESLEY HARMON 727-44-7088
licensed pimp
Member: Procurers Guild

He touched the lettering, then opened the door and entered the apartment to where Lorna waited. She'd have a drink ready, and she'd be ready.

THREE...

Sunlight was streaming in the window when Wes sat up on the edge of the bed and smiled down at Lorna. He yawned again, stretched, and touched her back, flesh that made "satiny" an inadequate, if not demeaning adjective.

With a small sound of protest, she tried to bury her head in the pillow. The sunlight turned her hair into a mass of flame that contrasted spectacularly with the sheet.

He grinned. Not every proc was lucky enough to represent his own siblings, and certainly not all of them, as he did. It kept things a lot more peaceful, with everything in the family. And the compulsory sterility injection every five years made the situation perfectly safe. Every postnubile female on the planet received the regular shots, infecting her with the latent, specialized disease called rubellina. It interfered with none of her normal processes—other than to sterilize her monthly eggs. Only mating slaves were permitted to bear children, and no woman in her right mind wanted *that* task. Not until after two or three recons, anyhow, and usually not even then. Despite the lifespan, deaths exceeded births. Even the hedon-screamers had pretty much shut up—at last.

Wesley and Lorna Harmon had been raised in a government creche, like everyone else. What they did after Rites was their affair. She had been waiting in his apt last night, with a drink and no questions.

24

"Work to do," he reminded himself, yawning again. He was tempted to leave her here. He hated to waken the girl among all his girls who had been born for bed; a law prohibiting her from leaving her natural habitat would not have been out of order, surely.

He rose, showered, and emerged from the stall before the rushing warm air had fully dried him. He slipped into a plain brown klamys and belted it with a piratically enormous black belt. Then he had to rush to catch the intercom.

"Wes?" The blonde-topped face was Geneviva's, the House maso-nymph.

"That nutty flagellant contract I had last night got all fobby and caught my whip in an antique electric fan. It—"

"A *what*?"

"You know—the old personal airconditioners, with propellors, like. It was my best one, too."

"The fan?"

"No, bug, the whip. I wanted to let you know I called and the whip man will be here in . . . one hour, Wes."

"Okay. Buzz off, then, while I see what I can get done meanwhile."

They blanked their screens and he returned to the bedroom of his office-living apt to rouse Lorna. He lifted her hypernubility from the bed and stood her on her feet. She blinked and objected, sleepily.

"Come on, Red, wake up, wake up. Another day, another contract. Time for working jays to have their breakfasts."

She yawned, managing in her irrepressible femininity to make even that a sensual act. Rubbing her eyes, she glanced around. "Hey—I wake up in the nicest places."

He laughed, urging her across the room. She bounced; a specialist in hefnerites, she had hormonated herself to a 42-D. "And me with the nicest people," he said. "Now pick up and start acting as if you woke up in your apt. I don't want any jealousy around here."

"Hey—that's right. You really came on strong last night. What happened?" She was gathering her clothing.

25

"Nothing," he said. "Nancee'll be fine, but it'll take a while. Honest. Now exit, exit."

The bundle of clothes she held against her dangling in sublimely ignored confusion, she paused with one hand on the door. "Coming over for breakfast, jacko?"

Her brother shook his head. "Too much business to take care of. I'll eat right here. Geneviva has a salesman coming over, and you might get a call. Exit!"

She smiled, made a kissing pucker with her lips, and exited. He made his breakfast call to the caterer, then went around behind his desk. He was checking the day's schedule when the catercloset dinged. He went over to the cabinet and opened the door to reach in for the little table—

and smoothed the vylon stocking over the gentle curves of an emphatically well-formed leg

dropped a token into the box and pushed his way into the crowded chopterbus, enjoying the softness and the perfume of the girl who brushed against him

—and paused, frowning, as he saw the little box in the center of the tray. There was nothing else. No dishes filled with food. No coffee. Just the box.

Closing his fingers hesitantly around it he paused, then picked it up and took it over to the desk. He let it rest there enigmatically while he settled himself in his chair. Cocking his head a little on one side in a mannerism he wasn't aware of, he studied the diminutive box. The letters had been printed there by hand:

Wesley Harmon 727-44-7088
P E R S O N A L

He lifted the lid—and froze in astonishment, staring. Resting in a bed of snowy fabric was a Star Pearl.

"What the HELL!" He poked at the fabric with a stylus. There was no note. Nothing, just the ridiculously expensive stone, the little crumple of white satin, and the box.

But dammit, nobody tosses these things around for free!

After staring at the gem for another devitalized moment, he stabbed at the visiphone with his finger. The face of the catering boy appeared, open in youthful innocence. Wes gazed at him a moment before speaking, with controlled casualness.

"Harmon on twenty. About this tray—"

The boy looked confused. "Tray? I'm sorry, Harmon, but your breakfast isn't quite ready."

Frowning, Wes glanced over at the tray, sitting there in the catercabinet. It hadn't arranged the Star Pearl on itself and climbed into the vutting thing and sent itself up!

"That's . . . odd. A tray just came up." Then he laughed. "Oh, well, it's empty anyhow. Probably something wrong with the controls down there, though. Better check the conveyor."

"Yessir. And your order will be right up."

Switching off the viz, Wes scratched his nose. *Am I being . . . taunted? And what the vutting effect can this thing have on me?*

He had never seen one of the stones before last night, and he certainly hadn't passed on a surreptitious query to the underworld, as Fallman had done. But two of his girls had received one of the things, and each had fragged out and had to be placidated. And he had become someone's favorite gun-target. And . . . yes. There seemed just as much connection between the jewels and the shootings as there was between what had happened to both Nancee and Phylis, last month.

What the vutting hell?

He replaced the lid on the little box and shoved it into his pocket.

"Scut! I'm a jay-girl expert, not a jeweler. What are they bothering me for?" Then, still frowning as he thought about it, he punched Central Infor.

"Give me the scrute on Star Pearl," he said, "the."

After a brief wait, a holopic of one of the stones appeared on the screen and he listened to the pleasantly feminine voice of the computer.

"Star Pearl the. Small oval-shaped gem of varying colors all contained within each stone; *not* a pearl. Usual size approx one inch length one-half inch width one-quarter inch depth. First appeared on Earth one-point-

27

seven years ago. Cost prohibitively high—current value desired?"

"Negative," Wes said.

"Small fortune, in parlance," the computer told him. "Were first sold by jewelry syndicate that refused to reveal source of supply. Good and accepted business tactic: no illegality no quarrel. Then indication arose of *possible-* connected resultant fantasies in human mind *perhaps* generated by Star Pearls. Probability of connection at present forty-nine-point-nine. Naturally, manifestations were limited and confined within small group due to cost of gems."

"Parlance," Wes said, tiring of the matter-of-fact flatness of the report. He gave his numbers and exhibited his credplate: translation into parlance was not covered in the Free Information Acts. He waited.

The voice that next emerged from the viz was male, nasal, and anonymous. The screen continued to show only the jewel.

"Some of the heifers who wore the jewels began fragging out, mindwise," the voice said. "Their semi-erotic world-bang fantasies made shrink-treatments necessary. The fantasies were nearly identical, but the Star Pearls were the only apparent connection: each woman had one. Since this happened only within a small group and a cozily wealthy one at that, they could make their complaints to Gov without publicity. The reaction of John Q, of course, would be that the rich were buying special legislation that would help no one but themselves: ref twentieth century. Gov met complainants halfway and banned import."

"That's all? No further legislation?"

There was a delay while Central Infor double-checked its answer. Fresh facts flowed into its banks each second.

"Negative. This was all Gov could do without violating Freewill."

Which told Wes that it was indeed all; otherwise he'd have got one of those "Classified" responses that meant more money and more trouble in obtaining the facts.

"All laws," Central Infor said sententiously, "are as

bad as they are good, but Man cannot do without them. The gems continue to come in, though. They're being sold underground. The syndicate has stopped handling them; this is positive. But no one could stop the desire for the jewels. They are prohibited, therefore they are popular, and their price has gone up. Addition: apparently not *all* possessors fob out."

"I hope not," Wes muttered. "Possession illegal?"

"Possession legal: Freewill. Importation illegal: Gov is investigating. Results negative."

"Finished," Wes said, and the screen blanked. Damn! He knew no more than he had last night. No one knew where the drilling things came from, or why, or how, and no one had as yet explained how the hell they went about creating their neural effect. And somewhere, someone was making a lot of money.

And I've got one. From an anonymous admirer? Not bloody likely!

The door chimed. Wes jerked his head, reoriented himself, and pushed the view button. He recognized the man and pushed Open. The door swung silently in to admit the slim man carrying the long suitcase.

"Good morning, Proc Harmon. Whipmaker's Guild; you wanted to see our latest creations this morning?"

"I recognize you—"

"Carlin."

"Yes, hello Carlin. One of my girls does need new equipment." He intercommed Geneviva at the same time as the catercabinet dinged again. "The whips man is here, sis."

Her reply was a delighted squeal. "I'll be right in!"

The merchant had laid his case on the desk and unfastened the catches. As he spread it open, the rich smell of fine leather filled Wesley's nostrils, and he paused on his way to the catercabinet. One thing Geneviva would not tolerate—plastic. It was real leather or forget it, whether she was wielding the whip or, as she preferred receiving it. She was a certified felinist, but she preferred taking to giving.

Wes went on over to the cc; this time the tray contained

his breakfast. Carlin shook his head to the offer of coffee, and Wes neglected his meal long enough to bend over the case.

"This appears to be a fine-quality assortment, Carlin."

"The best," Carlin told him unequivocally. "All our merchandise is handmade entirely, Harmon, with careful attention to the smallest details. Of course we charge for that, too, and for the real leather. We don't deal in machine-made plastics." He toned the words as if they comprised an obscenity. "Not only do the better class of jay-girls and their customers frown on such, but the Guild itself does. And for good reason. A machine can never assess human esthetics, and plastic will not satisfy the person who wants the smell and sound of good leather. It's one of the world's oldest fetishes. For those of us who wear mustaches and use razor and scissors rather than depils . . . consider how many aftershaves and men's scents contain the word 'leather' in the name.'"

Wes hadn't asked for a lecture, nor was he particularly ecstatted by leather or flagellation. Yet he did like the smell, and he made no argument. He'd heard the same more than once, from both Geneviva and her contracts— if less sufficiently put.

"Flagellation," Carlin said, with the air of a professor relieving himself of an aphorism, "is a uniquely and delicately personal matter."

"Um," Wes acknowledged, rounding the desk to un-cover his food. He looked us as Geneviva entered, wearing a clingy pink thing and an expectant smile. Her soft blond hair was done in a braid that swished back and forth on her back as she hurried to the case. She gasped in delight at the display.

"Oooooo . . . they're be-yoo-teefull!"

Carlin smiled with undisguised smugness. "Please take your time in your selection. I understand the importance of the right, *just* the right, choice."

Besides, Wes thought, *he's enjoying eyeballing Viva.* She was Justinely built: short, tiny, wide-eyed, with a mouth that could pucker and pout, and lachrymal glands that could spurt at the drop of a command.

Leaning over the case, she turned her head to fix Carlin with an ingenuously blue-eyed gaze. "Do you?"

Carlin looked at Wes. "Would you like me to wait in the hall while you test their efficacy?" He was moving doorward. "Most persons prefer testing their lashes in private."

Wes smiled. "Not necessary. I'm not a felinist."

Carlin looked strangely at him.

"Well, wait a minute," Geneviva said, straightening and looking pitiful. "Someone's got to help me test these out. Otherwise how could I possibly decide which is best?"

"Geneviva, I just don't—" Wes broke off and raised his brows at Carlin. Carlin nodded.

"I should be delighted to demonstrate the merchandise," he said.

She studied him. "Do you—know what you're doing?"

"I assure you I am not inexperienced," Carlin said, with enough firmness in his voice to make her smile and nod her agreement.

"Oh good, then." She lifted one of the whips, snapping it from her to uncoil its five-foot length. "Mmm . . . seems a bit stiff. The curve should be shorter." She rewound it and returned it to the case.

"You should have seen what happened to my best whip yesterday evening, Wes. He had this honest-to-gosh fan, an antique, and when he swung the whip back for about the tenth time . . ." She trailed off with a little shiver, rolling her eyes ceilingward as she reflected. "No, it was the *eleventh* lash. Anyhow, it rolled right up in that silly fan, and the blades just chewed it all up with the most awful noise! Those kooky antiquists! Honestly— I just can't understand people with such weird tastes."

Wes reached out to tug her braid. "You're lucky this didn't get caught."

She giggled, lifting out another whip. "Ah. This feels good." She tested the balance. "Positive. It's about the right weight."

"Shall we try that one?" Carlin asked.

"Oh yes, let's do." She handed him the whip.

"Now, hold on just a moment," Wes said, waving a

hand. "This is a business office, not a felinism chamber, and I don't fancy groans with my breakfast. You two go and run your performance tests in your apartment, Viva."

Geneviva's breathing had already quickened. "Right," she said, and she and Carlin departed. Wes sighed and tried to check the morning businessfax from his bank while he finished his meal. He didn't give another thought to Viva and the salesman. With the emergence of Freewill, both femlib and football had been considerably eclipsed. In the words of Morgan Drake in 2017, "every person now has the right to get his or her ecstats in his or her own way, and those who endeavor to interfere will be prosecuted, if not worse."

Harmon had totted up yesterday's earnings and expenditures and balanced the "books" when Carlin knocked lightly. He entered on invitation.

"She has made her selection," he said blandly. He wasn't even breathing hard when he laid the whip on the desk with loving care.

Wes nodded. "Good. I hope you two were able to restrain yourselves."

"She does bring out the natural felinism instinct," Carlin smiled, "but . . . yes. General Flagellant, Incorporated, if you please."

Wes signed the creditransfer and smiled at Geneviva, who was coming in as Carlin exited. She gave her brother a desolate look.

"I always get whipped by strangers and never by the man I love."

"Oh, come on, Viva. I used that blasted cat on you last year on your vacation, and all I proved was that sadism is not where I live."

"*What?*"

"Sorry," he said. "*Felinism.* Sadism's what the psychotic aspect of it's called. Hey, girl, you've got a contract in less than two hours. Come to think . . . it's Williston. Isn't he the one who uses the cat?"

She nodded. "And pays triple for the privilege. I'll be out of action for days."

32

"Then why in the drilling hell was this new lash so important you had to have it now?"

She smiled, reaching for the door. "Just an appetizer," she said. "I haven't had breakfast yet." And she and her childish face and figure left.

Grinning, Wes started working out the new schedule, filling in the holes created by Nancee's being put out of action. He was noting the calls he'd have to make, apologizing and reappointing, when the visiphone began winking at him. He activated the screen.

"Wesley Harmon, Licensed Proc. What's your kick?"

A woman's face smiled at him. "What else?"

He matched her smile with professional ease. "Specifically, then. We cater to every taste."

She rubbed her cheek with a slim, gloved hand. "Well, we don't want anything too unusual. Not a masochist or anything. Excuse me; 'we' is my partner and I."

"Good. My maso-nymph will be unavailable for several days. Is your partner male or female?"

"Male," she said, with a small smile. She was young, Harmon saw, younger than he'd guessed at first thought. Thirty or less. And good-looking. "We're in town for only for a few days, and we'd like to arrange a small orgy this evening. Small, seriously. It will round off our trip so nicely. We had in mind a General Practitioner who knows all the standard methodology and tricks. Oh—but not a delicate girl. My partner is quite heavy." She smiled again as she added, "A pretty girl, of course."

"I'm glad of that," Wes told her. "I'm afraid there is one taste we can't feed. We don't stock any uglies." He was examining the duty roster. One girl wasn't his idea of an orgy, small or otherwise, but he wasn't about to raise a semantic dispute with a contractee. Ouch—Nancee again, leaving a gaping hole in the schedule. Lorna would have to cover that one—but Brinny would take this, and this—and Geneviva this one, somehow.

"Lorna . . . Brinny . . ." he muttered, scanning down.

"Harmon? Did you say Lorna? We've been told about her. Is she indeed available?"

Well, that settled that. He nodded and showed the young

33

woman the 3-D photos of Lorna and her queensize personal equipment. "Yes. This is Lorna. She isn't a big-boned girl, but she is . . . ah . . . well padded, and can take considerable weight. I assure you it makes her no less active." He passed the photos across the screen's eye, one by one.

"Umm, a redhead—and she's gorgeous."

"I have to agree with that judgment," Wes said, thinking about last night.

"She will be just perfect for our needs, Harmon. Very sensuous-looking girl, very. Lot of flesh there. Would she be available at eighteen?"

"She can be. And she'll have had plenty of time to rest."

The woman laughed. "She'll need her rest!" She bent her head, then the gloved hand came up again, holding her credcase. Wes recorded the numbers, although the visiphone was recording. He also verified it, unobtrusively, and learned almost instantly that she had deposited a fat amount in a local bank. No trouble about collecting, then, but he registered a call on it, anyhow. He named the price; she nodded and shrugged.

"Suppose you just give the address and your preferences to my secretary," he said, and buttoned the robosec.

It beeped him when it had taken down all the information volunteered.

"Thank you," he told the gloved woman, "for contracting our services. The name, again, is Lorna."

"Thank you, Harmon." The woman blanked her screen.

A darned handsome gal, he thought, checking the preferences she *had named. But a liar, sure as I sit here. At least AC-DC, and I'd bet on it. Well, so is Lorna. There'll be no problem.*

The viz winked and beeped, and he activated.

"Wesley Harmon, Licensed Proc," he said, forgetting Lorna's new contract. "What's your kick?"

FOUR...

Lorna Harmon alit from the chopterbus and moved quickly away from it to escape the dust of its ascent.

Surrounded by the quiet of the suburban street, she checked the address she'd noted down. This promised to be an easy contract, and she was completely at ease and a little anticipatory as she stepped onto the proper pedway. Transferring to another at the junction, she followed the directions to the center of the block—and stepped off the pedway, frowning. The building appeared to be empty.

She had paid no attention to the hovercar until a voice called her name. She turned slowly. Apparently her contract intended taking her elsewhere—but not until she'd called in! She moved slowly over to the car, trying to see inside through the twilight dimness.

She stopped, stiffening, as the window dropped and the nasty snout of a little needler centered on her chest.

"Get in and don't make a sound," the female voice ordered. The door swung open. The gloved hand jerked the gun, waving her inside.

Moving carefully, glancing around and wondering just how far she'd get if she attempted to run—probably about five steps—Lorna obeyed.

"You can't—"

The needlegun was thrust into the softness of her hormone-enhanced bosom. "Yes we can. Shut up and get in."

She shut up and got in. And said, as she sat gingerly on the back seat, "This—this wasn't in the contract."

The woman gave her an acid smile that came entirely too easily to her handsome face. "We're rewriting this one. And don't go spouting about kidnap laws, Lorna dear. Just keep your hands right there in plain sight."

The car had already risen and was moving swiftly; the driver had not turned around. His hair, she noticed, was brown with a few streaks of gray, and he did not look particularly big. Which meant the whole contract was a hype. She sat still, chewing her lower lip, trying to find some clue to the situation. She tried to keep track of their changes of direction, too, peering intently out the window.

The woman beside her chuckled. "Look all you want. You won't remember a bit of it."

Lorna tried to be calm. "Why not?"

"Shut up, Harriet!" The driver's voice was an angry baritone.

Lorna had no idea why the thought came snaking into her mind. "Does—does this nonsense have something to do with Star Pearls?"

Harriet jerked. "Be quiet!" she snapped, and slapped her across the face. It was the break Lorna needed, and she used it. She grabbed for the gun. The woman screamed as Lorna wrapped one hand around the barrel and the other about Harriet's wrist.

The training of joygirls was not limited to sensuality, and Wes Harmon was even more thorough with his. Lorna worked the barrel of the needler rapidly in a pumping motion, ejecting the needle-packs. With a quick twist of her hands she tore the useless pistol from Harriet's hand and swung it up to strike at her head. It was then that the driver cut the aircushion control; the car dropped to the pavement with a sharp impact. Then he slammed on the brake. Both women shot off the seat to the floor. Lorna banged her head on his seatback as she fell.

Stunned, she was helpless enough for the woman to pin her.

The driver's voice came to her ears as though he were speaking in an echo chamber. "Tie her hands, Harriet.

36

Get her shoes off. It's a good thing you're a big heff and I had sense enough to help out, or she'd have knocked the hell out of you. She's no shrimp herself."

Groggy, Lorna struggled ineffectively as her wrists were secured together. She lay limply as her shoes were pulled off; she realized the uselessness of further resistance. She'd only angered them with her silly attempt. She lay still with her face against the car's rough carpeting. She heard a garage door, felt the car ease forward and stop again, and then its front door opened. Air and the lubricant-oil-dampness smell of garage rushed in as the door was opened near her head. Big or not, the man was strong. He dragged her out of the car and stood her on her feet.

He was blocky, not over-tall, and as un-criminal in appearance as he could be—which she knew was a meaningless categorization. His smile seemed to reflect genuine amusement. She didn't like his eyes.

"Take a good look around, jaygirl. It doesn't mean a thing. It's just an old garage. Your pimp can look it over in detail."

Harriet's fingers closed around Lorna's arm, pulling it up behind her. "Let's get going, Roland. The sooner you get this over with, the better my stomach will feel."

Lorna shivered. "What—" she began, but Harriet jerked at her bound wrists, and she subsided with a whimper. The garage floor was cold beneath her feet as they led her to a wooden door—to the outside. Surprised, she felt the caress of a cool breeze, heard the blithely cheerful sounds of crickets. Several feet away she saw the element-abused wall of an old house.

She had a choice: she could try to jerk away and run; she could scream until they stopped her; or she could accept it and try to be as tractable as possible in hope of lulling their attention. True, most would not have been aware of the choices under similar circumstances. But Lorna was not most, and she was Wesley Harmon's sister. She considered each before she spoke, trying to make her little laugh sound less nervous.

"You two seem fond of antiques. But I can't understand this—why didn't you ask for a maso-nymph? Are you so felinistic you have to have the illusion of *capturing* me?"

Harriet chuckled. "Not bad," she said. And that was all she said.

They led her to the sagging door of the old house. It opened with an aged creak, and she was thrust into a dusty hall. As they forced her along that corridor, she noted that there was no furniture in the rooms they passed. She shivered again and tried to think.

The man—Roland, Harriet had called him—opened a door, making Lorna squint as light rushed into the hall. Harriet hurried her forward so that the girl almost missed the top step.

"Easy, Harriet," Roland said, in irritation, and they helped the bound girl down the rough wooden steps. Fear rose in a wave that was a tightening in her stomach and a prickle in her armpits. Again she shuddered.

Then she heard the airgun sound, felt the pinprick in her arm, and turned her head to see Harriet grin at her as she drew back the exodermic needle. Lorna opened her mouth to shriek. Her mouth remained ajar, quivering, but the only sound she could produce was a throaty little rattle. The basement room seemed to dim and shimmer as her pupils dilated. Then her lights went out.

They let her fall, and for a moment Harriet and Roland looked at each other, across the crumpled body between them.

Harriet dropped to a feminine squat beside the unconscious girl and removed the bindings from her wrists. She rolled her over onto her back, found the polarizer in the form of a little gold button near the right shoulder of Lorna's dress, and reversed its field. The dress collapsed open. She looked up.

"Well, are you going to stand there or are you going to help?"

He shrugged. "I thought you might find it more interesting to undress her yourself, Harriet," he said mildly. And he smiled. "You might find it a bit easier without your gloves."

38

"Um." Harriet glanced down at her hands, then slipped off the gloves, revealing dark brown skin that contrasted paradoxically with the pale Cauc complexion of her face. Flexing her fingers, she grinned. "Harmon's going to look a long time to find the Cauc girl he contracted with."

Roland shrugged. "I think you overdid it. No one's that pale any more; we're all a mixed bag. How the devil your genes resulted in skin that dark with that straight nose and your lips, though, I'll never understand." He watched as she stripped the girl. "I think she overdid it, too. Topheavy."

Without care for the effect of the old cement floor on her flesh, they half-dragged the girl across the floor to where two thick iron posts stood a few feet apart, supporting the house above. They dumped her there while Harriet opened the metal box beside the left post. From it she took several lengths of rope. She tossed one to Roland, who knotted it to Lorna's left wrist while Harriet roped the other one.

"Make sure it's good and tight, Harriet. I don't want her downing things by pulling loose."

"Um."

Lifting the limp girl, Roland held her steady while Harriet tossed the ropes over a beam, then drew them down and secured them to the uprights. Lorna hung there, her head lolling to spill red hair down her bosom. She was forced to a standing position by the ropes, despite her unconsciousness. Roland and Harriet bound one of her ankles to each post. Roland chuckled.

"Like something out of the Inquisition," he said, standing back to regard the girl.

"Very nice," Harriet said quietly, brushing her hands briskly. She reached out. "It's a shame you have to ruin this nice piece of cake, Roland. She's gone to a lot of trouble to look like this. I could really go—"

"Harriet!"

She jerked her hand back, and he tempered his sternness. "The System's full of Lorna *bodies*," he told her, "and you'll have both the time and the money; you're in for several millions if you just follow my instructions when we've finished here. But right now we've got business." He was shrugging out of his jac. "Now you'd better get to the car. Unless of course, you want to watch."

Harriet headed for the stairs. "No, *thanks*. There are limits to what I'll do for money. I certainly don't have to see—this."

With one foot on the bottom step, she turned to gaze at the girl with a little frown. "I'd swear I've seen that girl before, Roland. She's familiar—"

"Not for long. Now get out of here and let me get this over with."

Harriet hurried up the steps—

and kissed him tenderly as her fingers slid down his strong body

crowded the other racecar to the electrail as his mighty machine rocked across the finish line

—and closed the door emphatically behind her, feeling gooseflesh. She brushed sympathy for the girl from her mind—without overmuch difficulty—and strode briskly to the back door.

As soon the the door closed, Roland returned his attention to the girl. He smiled, shaking his head, and began to speak to the air.

"She's right, you know," he muttered. "It really is a shame—" He paused, "listening" to the answer.

"Yes, I realize it's the only possible way to shatter Harmon's pattern . . . No, it hasn't solidified *yet*. I can detect a fragment of rejection, but you know I can't get it clear . . . I *know* you're not a magician, but logic should have told you that a network effect might trigger a Prime variant . . . *All right*. Don't release it until I'm ready, though. I'll tell you when."

He took the soldering iron from the open case and switched on its power. He stared at Lorna until the metal began to glow, then he moved toward the unconscious girl.

"You may release Balearic now," he muttered.

And he jerked, almost instantly. His cheeks sagged. His lower lip drooped open. His brow furrowed as he stared uncomprehendingly at the suspended body before him.

Spittle appeared at the corner of his mouth and began to inch down toward his chin. He giggled stupidly. Glancing down at the glowing iron in his hand, he looked back at the girl and chuckled, a rasping sound from the throat. He moved awkwardly forward, as though unaccustomed to his legs.

He raised the iron. It glowed white-hot. He began to use it.

The pain jerked Lorna back to consciousness. For just a moment she was silent, sniffing at the cooking odor, listening to the strange hiss. And then she began to scream. He laughed, a maniac's cackle, without interrupting his activity. Hysterical shrieks tore from her throat to mingle with his own insane screeches, reverberating from the cement walls.

He was far from finished with her transfiguration when she reached the absolute limit of pain reception and overloaded. She sagged again into unconsciousness.

Slobbering and chuckling idiotically, he continued his work.

After the first shriek, Harriet turned up the car radio to block out the noise. She puffed nervously, striving to reef serenity into her writhing brain. She waited, waited for him to complete his task.

It was taking a long time, she thought, and she shuddered. At last she heard a door slam. Glancing over her shoulder, she saw Roland stride into the garage, carrying the case. He appeared perfectly composed. He dumped the case into the back seat and slid in behind the wheel.

She switched off the radio; the sudden silence was deafening, almost a palpable entity. She shuddered again. "I . . . heard the . . . screaming even over the radio. How could you stand to do that to her?"

He turned to her with a bland smile, his eyes remaining flat. "What makes you so sure I did it?"

"Huh? What the vut do you mean? You—you were the only one there!" Her frown faded and an expression of comprehension appeared on her face. "Oh—I under-

41

stand. So far as anyone knows, you weren't even here."

Roland laughed softly, enigmatically. "Something like that." He backed the car out of the garage, took it up to two feet until it was away from the house, then lifted to eight hundred and gunned it.

FIVE...

Alone in his office, Wesley Harmon shoved back from his chair and ran his hands down into his pockets. And remembered the little box he had almost forgotten.

He pulled it out and lifted the lid to examine the stone again. It resembled a fine gem in the bright light; only that. And how much more was it? What did they expect him to do with it? *Hold it in my hot little hand and go round the bend? Not if I can help it!*

A sardonic smile pulled at his lips. *Maybe I should have left the whole* schmeer *to the Guild Protectors.* But no, his personal interest was too great. When the pimp's jays were also his own siblings, they were a double responsibility. So far as he knew, he was the only procurer with such a setup; there was no precedent, then, and no source of advice, even if he'd been the sort to ask advice.

It hadn't begun this way. He had left the creche with a pilot's rating and worked his way into a Deal: herding a bigcred's yacht between Earth and Luna. One by one, the kids had gone through Rites and left the government creche. He was big brother, the firstborn, the only male produced by an overworked mateslave; big brother was doing well. He wasn't even certain, now, which of them had solidified the concept of his heading a joygirl arrangement; they had all trained in that direction, almost exclusively. The idea had sort of grown, as they accumulated around him.

It was fortunate for Geneviva that it had come out this way. Otherwise she'd have ended up in a Whipping House, the destination of most certified felinist-receivers; "masochists," in the old terminology.

Leaning back, he stared at the ceiling, clasping his hands behind his head.

So what does it all have to do with Star Pearls? Who's selling the things—and why'm I being shot at? Nice questions, Harmon. Howcum no nice answers to match?

He glanced at the clock and smiled, thinking that by now Viva was ecstatically happy—and out of action for days, even though he'd damwell put her into the Doctor. He wondered how Lorna was making—

—and the visiphone winked at him. He leaned forward and activated. The screen remained black as the woman's voice issued from the speaker.

"My, you do work long hours, don't you? Good—that saves us time and trouble."

"What kind of trouble, and why are we view-blanked?" He recognized the voice. "I've never had a complaint about Lorna, but if—"

She laughed. "Oh, we have no complaints about that sweet heifer. She screams *beautifully*."

His blood pressure lurched upward. "Hey—wait a min. You're not felinating that girl—she's not trained for that!"

The voice became flat and sinister. "Make that past tense, Harmon. She's just been to school."

"You goddam stash—if you've harmed that girl I'll have you slapped in prison for the next century! *After* I knock hell out of you."

"Not likely," she said, and then she snapped, "Look, paisano, I haven't time to argufy. Be sure this goes on your recorder so it doesn't get lost. 20035 Wertham Road. Don't hurry; she isn't going anywhere."

The set had hardly clicked off before Wes was jamming down the red button. A very alert-looking man stared at him.

"Guild Protec Service. What's the emergency?"

Wes gave him the address and a fast rundown, then added, "Bring an ambulance." Then he slapped off and

44

yanked off his coat. Jerked open a desk drawer. Took out his holstered gun and hung it around himself. Struggled into the coat and adjusted the harness as he ran to the door. He took the hall at a dead run.

In the elevator, he jabbed X(press) and cursed because it didn't respond instantly. Then he was up, and out, and racing to his car. The boy called something; Wes ignored him and shot up off the roof without bothering to check other traffic. Buttoning Auto, he took his hands off the wheel. The express beam could handle the car at speeds much higher, safely, than he.

He unholstered his gun, checked the cylinder, and tucked it back. The sleek car shot along the beam it had chosen automatically, after making certain it was unoccupied. Automatically, Wes shoved a cigaret in his mouth, reviewing the brief conversations with the woman. Dammit, that was the hole in this business. Some of them preferred anonymity, and so long as they flashed their cred and it checked out at the bank, he didn't care what their names were. People were easy enough to trace via their cred—but he had the hideous feeling he was going to learn that that card was a ringer.

Was there a connection with the damned jewels again? Three of the girls down, now—and what kind of brother could protect them no better than this? He blasted out smoke in angry huffs, watching the traffic around him without seeing it. Never mind that it wasn't his fault; he couldn't shake off the feeling of guilt.

Maybe I'd better close down for a while as a safety measure. Lord, we're moneyed enough to close down for twenty years!

The warning light flashed. The car began slowing, and Wes took over to effect a beam-transfer. Then he punched Maximum and Auto again and waited in sweating tension while the machine left the city.

The building was old, very old, but the address was still just visible, glowing on the roof. The car lurched as it tried to make speed in its descent, meanwhile avoiding the trees. He took over, landing beyond the house. Then he was running as silently as he could, gun out, hanging close to the bushes.

He glanced back as he neared the building. No sign of the Protectors, but he could just hear the shriek of a siren; the ambulance was coming on full. The clearly moonlit night provided no cover between him and the house, now, and he surveyed it from the edge of the trees.

Then he ran like hell, gun up and ready. The only sound was the slap-slap of his own feet, followed by the creaking of the porch as he reached it without being fired upon. Cautious once again, he turned the outdated knob and pushed at the old wooden door. It swayed inward on creaking hinges. Inside, the place looked as deserted as the overgrown grounds. He saw the line of light down the hall, near the floor.

Moving as quietly as possible, he edged toward the light, which he saw marked the bottom of a door. Again he twisted a knob with slow care, again he crouched as he shoved an old, old door inward. Nothing. No sound, no scuffle or voice or hornet-flurry of darts. Just steps, going down into a lighted basement.

He went down, slowly, crouching, the big revolver ready. He was two steps from the bottom when he saw her. His stomach muscles convulsed. He felt nausea and bile boiling up. His mind recoiled, tried to seek sanctuary in a lunge toward unconsciousness or insanity. He fought it.

"My . . . *god*. Even her FACE!"

Hideously scarred with leaking wounds that had blistered and bubbled and popped even as they'd been seared there . . .

No. He couldn't believe it. No. It was impossible. It wasn't she it wasn't it wasn't—but the downstreaming red hair identified her beyond question.

"Lorna. Lorna! *Lorna!*"

The burning blazing searing light beat upon his eyeballs without warning. The walls shuddered, trembled, bowed and seemed to crumble under the onslaught of cataclysmic turmoil and he was staring into a hell, a holocaust of great

46

and towering buildings that shook and collapsed grace-
fully, slow-motionly, until they broke off and crashed in
bounding shards onto the smoking ground and fire belched
from the lips of sudden gaping fissures that poured molten
lava across the delicately ornate mosaics of courts and
plazas. Dark clouds raced across the thundering, shud-
dering sky, but even their overshadowing could not blot
the bulbous horror on the horizon.

Wesley knew that he was watching a collision of planets. Worlds on which people had lived and loved and made love and dreamed and now died in monstrous armageddon. But all, all of it flowed into his mind only from around the central figure in the satanic panorama. She stood serenely there, in the midst of nightmare. A woman of incredible beauty. A sheer, flowing gown of red caressed her unconditionally magnificent figure; delicate gems of many colors sparkled and shown in hair whose blackness was deeper than the clouds above her. And her eyes . . . It was the eyes that held him, that pierced and probed and mocked him, staring into his with fixed purpose he could not decipher.

He cried out, and suddenly he was free of the spell and his revolver was roaring, spewing .45-caliber slugs into the vision.

The hammer clicked on an empty chamber and smoke spiraled up from the barrel.

The woman remained, standing, her gown billowing slightly. Only her expression had altered. Now he could discern a slight, but triumphant smile. Just one glimpse—

and then it was gone. All of it. The hellish landscape and the staring woman, vanished, swallowed up into the same nothingness that returned the basement walls to where they had always stood.

Harmon slumped back against the wall by the stairs, panting. With one shaking hand he wiped the sweat from his face. He was covered with it, his clothes wet. Then he became aware of the voices.

"Harmon! Harmon!"

Feet pounded, upstairs. "Harmon! Are you here? Are you all right?"

Grim-faced, efficient-looking men poured down the steps, their guns out and up and ready. With them came two others, in white uniforms. They rushed to the dangling body between the posts.

The gray-haired Protector slipped his gun back into its holster and grasped Wesley Harmon by the shoulder.

"What happened here, Wes? What were you shooting at?"

"I saw it! My God, I *saw* it!" Wes was trembling; he shook his head dazedly. The revolver swung at the end of his arm.

Furrowing his brow, the other man examined Harmon's face intently. His grip tightened as he glanced over at the gruesome body.

"I—know how you must feel, Harmon. Don't look at it. *Look away*. It's a good thing you didn't hit her with that monster gun you carry—there might still be some life left in her. Who was she?"

Wes stared at him. "I wasn't talking about her. She—she's got to be dead. But—I saw what those girls saw. The ones who had the Star Pearls."

The Protector nodded, patting him on the shoulder. "Right. You're in shock. It could happen to any man, under these circumstances."

"Dammit, Blake, I'm not in shock!" Wes rose to his feet and glared at the man. "I saw a woman, standing in a burning world, and somehow I just started shooting at her. She—she's an enemy . . ." He trailed off, running a hand through his hair. "I don't know. I guess . . . it must have been shock. Reflex action."

"Blake! This woman's still alive."

"Well, don't *talk* about it, get her to a hospital!" Blake strode to where the whitecoats were cutting loose the mutilated girl.

Apathetically, still trembling a little, Wes watched Blake move away. His eyes wandered—and saw the two dark, crumpled shapes on the floor. They were almost invisible against the dirt, like hand-sized black spiders. He glanced around furtively before stepping forward. With a casually swift motion he scooped them up and slipped them into his pocket. He turned back to the steps.

"I'm going outside, Blake. My stomach—I need some air."

Blake looked around. "Hold on, I'll come along." He turned from the man who was softly dictating his report. As they walked through the dusty hall, Wes ejected the cartridge casings from his gun and began pushing new bullets in. He shoved the pistol into its holster as he and Blake stepped out onto the porch. The ambulance still hovered above a billowing cloud of dust; there were three other cars.

Wes glanced at the man beside him. "Think I'm going to do something desperate?"

Blake hunched stocky shoulders as he thrust his hands into his pockets. He gazed at Wes a moment before nodding.

"I know you are. I'm not a Govman, but I'm cop enough to know when a man's turning killer."

"That's my sister. What would you do in my place?"

Blake sighed, then stepped quickly out of the way as the two whitecoats rushed by with the girl, cocooned in a plastic balloon full of anesthetic antiseptics. They hurried her into the ambulance, which began to rush upward even before the door was closed. Siren ululating, it rushed back toward the city.

"I don't know," Blake admitted. "I don't pimp for my sister; I don't have one. If I did, I'd probably feel the same way you do. But I wish you'd give it more thought. We can do the job, Wes, and a lot more efficiently. We're trained for it."

"No. I want my bullets in their guts." He paused, and there was an undertone of savagery in his voice when he went on, biting out the words, "I don't want them to die efficiently, Blake. When I kill them, they'll know they're being killed. I want to make it just as slow and dirty as I can."

"Wes—"

"She was beautiful, Blake. Warm, all for love, My god, they couldn't have done anything more horrible. She was burned, *burned*, Blake, a little at a time with something

49

like a branding iron. It took all my control to keep from putting a bullet into her head just then when they carried her by. The—the only thing that kept me from going insane down there was—was what I saw. Inferno. Armageddon." He jerked in a violent shudder. "And the way that ambulance door slammed . . . final . . ."

"Listen, Wes Harmon, you've got to let—"

"Blake, I want the Guild to arrange a caretaker for the business." Wes started down the steps; Blake followed. "I don't know how long I'll be gone. Until I find them. I want the girls taken care of."

"Wes—" Blake waved a hand and gave it up. "All right, idiot. How do we explain about your leaving without seeing them? You do mean now, right now?"

"Right now," Wes nodded. "Uh—have your psych department work out something to cover our disappearances, Lorna's and mine, and they can brief me when I come back. I do *not* want the others to learn about Lorna, not right away. The shock would be—too much. But let my accountant know the truth. Whatever isn't covered by insurance can be paid out of my cred. Um . . . while you're at it, close the business down for about a month. Maybe I'll be back by then. The girls can use a vacation, anyhow. And *watch* them, Blake. Tight."

"Positive. One's a maso-nymph, isn't she?"

"Right. Geneviva. And that's not just a business act—she needs her mistreatment. See to that, too. Lord, they all live for soaring."

Blake produced a nobac cigar and crammed it into his mouth. "We can handle it," he said around the black cylinder as he fired it. "What's the time limit, Wes? Think about it. What happens if you—"

"Get killed?" Wes looked at him without concern. "That'd make everything easier. Just tell them I got it in an accident. If Lorna doesn't recover—"

"Come on, Wes, you know she will."

"—give 'em the same story. They're all covered by Guild insurance and personal policies, and they've got cred piled up you wouldn't believe. They're all financially—listen, that's enough. You know what to do. I'm tired of talking." He grinned at the Protector. "I'll call you when I'm back."

"Wes—"

"I mean *if* I get back," Wes called, over his shoulder. He was already trotting down the drive to his car. Blake stood there and watched it shoot aloft, U-turn in the middle of the air, and race toward Megaterra.

SIX...

Roland worked his way through the crowded terminal until he reached the railing where Harriet stood. He handed her the plascase.

"Here're your tickets. Don't lose them."

Without bothering to reply, she tucked them into the pouch at her thick belt. Tall for a woman, she dressed her abundant figure with fashionable care, and femininely. Her voice, too, was melodious and feminine, low, and a little throaty.

"Did you check your baggage?"

"Of course. It's probably on the ship already." He studied her face. "Feel better with your own skin back?"

She touched one brown finger to her cheek and caressed the brown flesh. "Yes! I wish they'd make the stuff so it could be worn awhile without removing it. Taking it off every night and having to put it back on every morning was a rectal pain."

"I suppose," he said, with his usual smile: small, thin. "But it was effective. It was necessary for you to establish Caucoloid, rather than Afraloid identity here, and you should be perfectly safe from Harmon or anyone else. Anyhow, the chemicals that gave that makeup stability would have clogged your pores if you'd left it on too long. It it ever dried conpletely we'd have had to have it taken off by a doctor—along with your admirable skin."

She gave him a distasteful look. "You should be an

52

expert on skin problems. I just don't see how you had the guts to do that."

He laughed softly. "You would be most amazed at how many guts I have. But shut up about it. We'll just not mention it again, not even aboard ship, in or out of Earth's territorial limits. Not at *all*, Harriet. Let's just hope that we achieved our goal: that Harmon is a raving lunatic by now. Certain others connected with this enterprise are of the opinion that he would become a . . . problem, if we have not stopped him."

"Hmp. GunTek did a magnificent job of failing to stop him!"

Roland shrugged, gazing steadily at her. He always looked directly at her, and the eyes, their expression, their flatness, never changed. "And I know why, Harriet, but it is not necessary that you know. Just assume that you are working for a bug crazy enough to pay you several millions when the job is all finished. Naturally you cannot have it *now*; one needs some assurance that you will not back out."

"I have no complaints," she told him, looking away from his eyes. "The advances are more than sufficient." She gazed across the great terminal. Through the immense transparent dome that covered the entire building, she could see the gleaming shape of the big Mars liner, in the process of loading passengers and cargo. Glancing down to the main floor, she winced and twisted her mouth when she saw the near-naked woman. She moved along at the end of the chain attached to her collar. Neither she nor the man leading her paid any attention to the distasteful glances from the crowd that hastily made way for them. No one touched the woman.

"Good god! How could that downer have the gall to bring his mateslave in here?"

Roland surveyed the pair with mild interest. "I suppose one has to move the creatures about once in a while. It is foolish to try to pretend that such women don't exist. Perhaps Gov permits it as a—warning."

"Ugh!" Harriet wrinkled her nose. "Who needs a warning? Just the thought of a bellyful of babies is—nauseating.

We have Freewill now, and the sexes are equal, and that sort of thing should be *stamped out!*"

Roland laughed, lifting one booted foot up onto the rail. His glistening metallic klamys fell away from a leg sheathed in black hose.

"Well put, Harriet, and with ridiculous logic." He shook his head. "You must endeavor to pretend to be intelligent enough to know why the race survives, after all. When the League established Freewill, you women chose the r-injection as if it were going to be discontinued within a week. The birthrate plummeted. Good! But after a while someone was smart enough to realize that they had to establish permanent slavery for any woman who showed the slightest inclination to bear children. So they do, all of them, and as many as possible. Reconditioning prevents their becoming what they would have years ago— fat sows." He chuckled. "The truth is, Harriet, that I would not be talking with you if mateslaves did not exist."

"You—you sound like you're apologizing for them!"

Still smiling, he shook his head. "You sound like a frieden. You'd be pale if you were able, wouldn't you?" He chuckled. "No, no. It isn't necessary for me to apologize for anyone. I assure you, I am not one bit concerned about the human race."

She gazed thoughtfully at him, running her tongue back and forth between her lips. He glanced at her, then waved a hand.

"Look around you! Do you see anyone else who is? There's no overpopulation problem any more, because no one cares. Except that." He nodded in the direction of the mateslave, now vanishing on the other side of a mass of people.

"Oh, hell!" she snapped. "This kind of talk makes me sick. Let's get aboard so I can find a nice little heifer to play with. "We've got a long, long cruise ahead of us. And if that creature's aboard, I swear I'll stuff her out an airlock or something, first chance I see."

She flung herself away from the railing and headed for the autostairs.

Roland followed, smiling. "So we have a long cruise.

54

Why is that a factor? You don't seem to have any trouble piloting your own ship, alone."

"That's business," she threw back over her shoulder. "I don't let anything interfere with that. But someone else is piloting this crate, and it'll be full of girls. I'll go fobby if I don't have my share."

He walked behind her, studying her back thoughtfully. Other men did, too, but for entirely different reasons.

I: BEGINNING

It took him several weeks to become adjusted to the gravity of the new planet. During that time he remained in or near the ship where it rested in the little canyon at one end of the sprawling valley. This was the end of it, and perhaps it was a beginning. The ship had possessed only fuel sufficient to make the landing here. As a matter of fact, there hadn't been quite enough; it could not have been called a wholly soft landing.

He was alone with eternity. It was worse than unpleasant, but after a while he grew accustomed to that, too. The adjustment was more brutal than to this world's gravity. But he had hope, now. Periodically he examined the valley with the ship's telescopic visor, checking the activities of the creatures he had selected. They would have to do, rough beasts or not. Only their kind appeared capable of the desired evolutionary progression. He discounted the other primate forms: they were dead-ending already.

"So am I," the Survivor thought somberly. "An Undead end. I'll watch them live and die for a thousand years, and they'll think I'm a god."

Dubious honor! He shuddered at its emptiness. But he shook off the depression as he had shaken off everything else, and he lifted the slim gun and left the ship again.

A tropical mist hung like a curtain of gauze over the warmth of the valley. Walking down the ramp, he turned onto the rocky trail that led to the jungle. There was a watering place, several miles away, that was used by the primates when they descended from their caves.

After an hour and more of pushing his way through the dripping foliage, he parted the ferny leaves and looked down on the waterhole. And watched it and waited, with the patience of one who has all the time in the world. This world. One of the autochthonous anthropomorphs would come along, eventually. He waited. Listened in silence to the sounds of insects and small animals and bright-plumed birds. Somewhere off in the jungle, he heard the full-throated bellow of some larger beast, one of the predators . . . the four-legged predators. He waited.

He did not stir when the figure appeared, shuffling down the well-worn path on the far side of the pool. The Survivor spent many minutes raising the gun; these creatures were prodigiously, uncannily perceptive. He sighted carefully. He squeezed. The gun's hiss was no more than his own aspiring breath, but the primate stumbled instantly and fell, just at the water's edge. The Survivor ran, circuiting the pool.

Hoisting the simian to his shoulder, he strode back into the jungle toward his ship.

Once inside, he adjusted the creature on the table. He had long since prepared everything he would need; it had been ready to function the moment the ship was completed. He was merely carrying out the final operating mechanics. Carefully adjusting the helmet on the unconscious primate, he inserted the prism and depressed the white button. The prism scintillated with a thousand shades of color. A vibrating hum flowed from the machine, faded, went silent. The prism had vanished.

He removed the helmet and waited for the primate to waken.

It did at last, blinking its yellowish-edged eyes and making gutteral sounds through flabby lips. Raising its long arm, it stared at the fur-covered length of it for several silent moments.

The Survivor ran his fingers through his beard, suddenly aware that he was sweating.

"I'm sorry," he said. "It was the best I could do. None of the others had any chance of evolving properly. I don't know which of us is better off. I'm the only one of my kind, too."

He turned abruptly to cross the cabin to the open airlock. Gazing silently out, he wondered if it had been worth the trouble. He had lost the only things of importance to him—all of them. When she had died, they were all he had left. Now he had only this cargo of memories.

The primate sat up, clumsily, and worked out a throaty-growly sound from its throat, just as clumsily. Dropping to the floor, it shuffled toward the tall, straight man. It raised its hairy paw to pat his shoulder in a gesture that was either ludicrous or—pitiable. Or perhaps piteous.

"This good. No talk like me, but good. Think not same, but work. We succeed."

The days following were filled with sufficient endeavor to keep the Survivor's mind from his own problems. He was fortunate in having bagged a male, first try. With its residual instincts, it was able to help him in trapping others. A female first, of course.

The gradually increasing clan outgrew his little canyon and flowed out to set up villages in the great valley. They had the knowledge of firemaking that the original primates had not possessed, and they were capable of organization into cooperative units—capable and eager and gregarious. What the Survivor began to expect began to occur as their minds became absorbed in the simple matter of existence and mating.

Years passed.

The tribes spread throughout the valley, and their memories of the Survivor faded from the truth, merged into myth. He became god, then God, in the sacred canyon at the head of the valley. This became a concrete fact in their minds on those occasions when it was necessary for him to break up the tribal conflicts that held danger of becoming suicidal wars. The flame from his heavier weaponry became fire from heaven. The language devolved, conforming with their vocal abilities, and the Old Words were known only to the shaman-priests that rose among them.

The Survivor watched the first generation die, watched

the next rise to take its place. Years drifted past, and he was alone. The sacred canyon became a mythical garden of great beauty. Naturally, it was forbidden to mortals.

The Survivor laughed, not without bitterness. "Such is the hell of the gods!"

SEVEN...

As the car rode the traffic beam back to the metropolis, Wes examined the objects he'd picked up from the floor of that basement of horror. He unfolded one of them, examining the wrinkled leather. No; it was reel-hyde.

The glove was too small for a man, unless he were a very small man. Besides, it was more a woman's cut, and he remembered the gloved hand of the woman who had called to make the contract with Lorna. He squinted, then raised the glove to examine the stain. It was a flesh tone, a little lighter than his own skin. Slightly greasy, just a little.

She rubbed her cheek when she called me the first time. Her cheek. I might not have noticed, but on the little viz-screen every action's exaggerated. She rubbed her cheek. And this came off. Makeup, flesh-toned. She isn't Cauc, then. But it could be about anything else . . . no, it can't! Not Oriental: not those eyes and nose! Dark, then. India, Africa, S.A.

"Dammit! How am I going to recognize her? She's brown or black, and I saw her as Cauc, and all I have to go on is her voice."

He wondered: what would Blake do? He knew what the end result would have been, had he given Blake the nod to investigate: a neat liquidation with no corpi, dilecti or otherwise. Spaced, probably. But this was just

59

too vutting personal to put into the cold hands of a murder squad.

Back to the problem. Had Blake found the gloves, what would he have looked for? Labels. Wes smiled and looked for labels. The tiny imprint within the glove stood out like a neon sign, now he was seeking it: F.O.M.

Federation of Mars!

Maybe it was an import, bought on Earth, but it was a lead.

He watched the metal and extruded silica and pressed-refuse towers of Megaterra drawing nearer as he pondered.

She was not Caucasian; not predominantly, that is.

She had a male partner. She *might* be Martian.

He went back to the viz conversations. Was she merely being insulting when she called him *paisano*? It was Italian for peasant, sure sure. But no Italian would give herself away with a lapse into the old tongue. Nor would she use Cauc makeup as a disguise; more like black.

The woman knew he lived in MegaTee; she wasn't deriding that, not the most sophisticated city in the System, not to mention Gov center of the Terran League!

Lesbie. They often referred to heteros as peasants. And on Mars . . . it was clinched, then. He remembered, from years back. That little brown man who had made some crack about Nancee's acting as though she were a lez; "acted 'sif she thought me just one more paisano," he'd grunted, trying for a rebate. It hadn't worked, of course, but Wes remembered, and now he was very grateful to the little chiseler.

She was black or brown, and she was lesbie, and she was from Mars. She had a partner who wouldn't show his face—maybe because Wes would recognize him? (Maybe because he was senior, and smart!)

The best place to begin the search was the tourist hotels—after a call to Spaceport Center.

Grinning, he shoved the gloves back into his pocket—and touched the little box. *The damned Star Pearl!*

Why do I keep carrying this abomination around? And what's so flaming important about them? So I've got one. So I had the vision, too. So I shot up six cartridges and I didn't go over the edge. So——shaking his head, he lit a cigaret and stuck it between his lips to keep from chewing them——

——and took his hands from the steerbar and stared in astonishment at the butt in the ashtray. *I just lit that thing!*

A cold hand touched him as he glanced out the car windows. Where——was——he?

Parked. In front of a blocky domed building, an old one. The Metropolitan Planetarium. Twenty miles from where he'd been when he lit that cigaret—that one, that butt there—and he had no memory of driving, of auto-punching this destination. But here he was. And the engine was silent. *Why?*

He sat quietly, watching the crowds moving in and out of the building, and he was suddenly aware that he had entered into something far bigger and far more baffling than "just" a case of a sadistic smuggler. His fingers touched the pocket that held the Star Pearl. Was it the cause of the blackout? Was the prismatic little gem responsible for what he had seen in the basement of the old house? The woman . . . the planets hurtling together . . .

Worlds in collision. . . .

An intangible essence of triumphant accomplishment feathered across his brain and he knew with absolute certainty that it had not been his, *his* own, *reaction.*

He had felt it before. No! He had seen it! The look on the woman's face when he had pumped a full cylinder of slugs into her without touching her. And one thing was certain: there was a reason for his brief fugue. He had come here, to the planetarium, for a reason.

Whose reason?

He had no idea whether he would find an answer inside, or another equivocal clue. But he had to go in. Anything was better than this frustrating impasse. *That horror did affect my mind. I guess I'm lucky I didn't go right over the edge.*

He stepped out onto the edge of the pedway, checked carefully to be certain he was in a legal parking zone, and closed and locked the door. Then he took a deep breath and strode up the broad steps to mingle with the throng entering the planetarium. They were mostly adults, of course, though here and there he noticed a Sponsored Juvenile—a Sponje—accompanied by the strange throwback adults who contracted to raise and be accountable for children outside the creche.

Inside the great building, Wes located a seat among the many that encircled the broad platform with its array of apparatus. Within two or three minutes the lighting dimmed, then faded to near-darkness. The spectacular show began, drawing awed gasps and murmurs from those about him: those who had never been in space and were totally uninterested in venturing offearth—eighty percent of the audience.

He listened to the speaker, seeking some useful bit of infor that would be new to a licensed space pilot—or a clue to why he was here. None came, and a feeling of depressed futility slid over him. More disgusted even than bored, he slumped in his chair to watch without interest as an illuminated ring rose from the platform.

The friendly, just-a-plain-man-folks voice of the lecturer permeated the room from well-spaced amplifiers.

"All this has been most colorful, of course. It was designed for stimulating edification; naturally, it is not the planetarium's intent to bore you."

Bullshit, Wes thought angrily, remaining resolutely bored.

"Therefore I do hope that you will not find this final exhibit without interest, even though it is small in scope. The subject matter, however, is tiny in scope itself, a fitting match for the exhibit."

Harmon glanced around disgustedly at those who supplied, dutifully, the chuckles the speaker waited for.

"Our subject is asteroids. Asteroids. The first was discovered in 1801, long ago and yet surprisingly recent within the great length of our recorded history. The discovery of the asteroids was a bit of mathematical wizardry —doubly so, when you remember that there were no computers at the time." (Murmurs.) "Even earlier, in 1772, a man named Johann Bode devised a geometrical succession that was subsequently labeled 'Bode's Law.' It accounted for all the planets then known and predicted later discoveries. Unfortunately, it also postulated the existence of a planet that was never found."

Exhibit: concentric circles formed by pulsing lights of different colors against a black background.

"The position indicated on Bode's table at two-point-eight proved obstinately and decidedly empty. This is the great gulf that separates relatively near Mars from far Jupiter. Eventually, a man named Piazzi *did* discover an object in that area, and named it Ceres. But it hardly conformed with Bode's tabulations and predictions. Ceres is only four hundred eight miles in diameter, hardly sufficient to balance Bode's Law. The assumption was made that there must be many such planets, and such was the case. Soon there followed the discoveries of Pallas, of Juno, and Vesta.

"The finding of asteroids became something of a fad, and ultimately some two thousand were annotated."

Harmon was surprised to find that he was leaning forward, listening intently. His mind had grasped the edge of something, something he was sure was of vital importance, though not as yet clearly defined. His eyes remained on the luminous ring as the lecturer spoke on.

"Obviously, not even two thousand specks in space were enough to verify Bode's Law. Most asteroids range *down* from the *relative* hugeness of Ceres to less than a mile in diameter, provided one is willing to refer to a chunk of rock as possessing diameter. To further complicate the matter, these objects were distributed over an area of three-hundred-forty millions of miles from the inner to the outermost orbit."

stupid little creature talks as if that were some sort of great distance

"Eventually, astronomers arrived at a bit of scientific rationalization that appears the only sensible conclusion, and here the matter still stands."

Around the luminous ring two spots of light moved, side by side. *not quite so close; these stupid little creatures are off thousands of mi*

"If we assume that Ceres and Juno are major orbits of the asteroid groups, we note that they intersect at one point, approximately. At this point they are very close to an equal plane of their relation to the ecliptic. It is believed that their curious orbits can be explained by assuming that at one time the asteroidal area was occupied by binary planets. Twinned worlds, if you will. Each followed an identical orbit; each rotated about a common center of gravity. All was well with them."

The two circles of light spun on around the circle. And then there appeared another light-circle, huge by comparison. The two smaller dots began to waver slightly.

"Some outside source—possibly . . . Jupiter?—began to affect one or both of the binaries to such an extent that they developed individual orbits."

The supports tilted apart, separating the luminous ring into two interlocking circles. Something within Wesley Harmon screamed along the corridors of his inner mind, crying out for recognition, as he watched the spots of light moving, separately now, each on its own ring.

"Inasmuch as these orbits were variations of the original one, they intersected at two points." The speaker paused for dramatic effect. "It was inevitable that, eventually, a disastrous meeting occur. It did."

The voice pounded like a hammer in Harmon's brain as he watched the two spots of light, representing two mighty planets, two *worlds*, moving closer and closer together. Then—

—he was hurtling toward them and the universe was aflame with the majestic expanse of the myriad constellations forming a glittering backdrop for cataclysm. The moving spots of light became disks. The ring vanished. He was there, at the death of two worlds! Remembered visions splashed into his mind. Towering mountains stretched up in their attempts to pierce the sky, embracing verdant valleys and green plains laced by cool unpolluted rivers that stretched their fingers to windswept seas. Now the disks took on depth, becoming spheres with clouds fluttering and boiling across their surfaces, obscuring the continental features.

("resulting in a planetary collision that in turn resulted in the total destruction of both worlds")

The paths converged with agonizing slowness. The planets reeled beneath him, their flaming atmospheres boiling in torment. Crimson wraiths curled around the doomed worlds. Minute silvery objects pierced the tortured clouds, streaming insignificant trails of flame and reaching in desperation for the distant stars. One by one, they were dragged back. Losing their velocity, they curved gracefully, then plunged back into the maelstrom.

The planets stumbled from their orbits, swinging, then hurtling toward one another. Titanic ruptures belched forth on the surface of the nearer world. The atmospheric envelopes bulged and stretched toward each other. Closer, and closer.

The elongating globes seemed to touch lightly for an incredible eternity of horror that merged into a moment of monstrous dissolution. Wesley Harmon watched the living planets die in ultimate cosmic horror. Inferno exploded: a universal scream that knifed out across eternity, that pounded against his mind with unrelenting urgency.

She died. They died. They all died. The worlds died.

The lights flared up amid pandemonium in the auditorium. All eyes were wide, fastened on the tall, muscular man who was standing with fists clenched and face dripping sweat—a face that bore the expression of one who has walked with Dante and seen purgatory and the utter hell beyond. Shaking violently, Harmon knew that the scream had come from his own throat, that it had echoed millions upon millions of screams, torn from horrordying throats time out of mind—and he knew who and what he was.

He had not seen a planetarium exhibition. The two luminous rings were still interlocked in the center of the auditorium. They were all the place had contained, aside from the staring people. What he had seen had been the real thing: Sodom and Gomorrah and Tyre and Nineveh and Hiroshima and Nagasaki: all were pale imitations of death and destruction on an unthinkable scale.

The lecturer turned up his volume, shouting to establish order. "Please be seated! Citizens—oh, good god, the program's *ruined*! Ushers! *Ushers*! Remove that man and detain him for the authorities!"

Remove? Detain? Authorities? *These*? DETAIN

Wes looked about the hall. A group of guards was rushing down the aisle toward him. Others emerged from doors around the central platform.

Horrified spectators melted back or were bowled over as he leaped out into the aisle, his gun in his hand. Huge-eyed ushers dived for cover. He ran. Up the aisle. Toward the exit. Passed through the big double doors, many voices shouting behind him. Slammed the doors. Aimed. His revolver roared, roared again, sending slugs tearing into the locking mechanism. It jammed. He heard the screaming and shouting behind him as he raced through the lobby. But no one stood in the way of a man with a face like *that*, smoking gun or no. Unmolested, he gained the front door and cursed because his legs would not carry him down the front steps as fast as he commanded—

—twisted the key in the car and slapped buttons: Ignition. Semi-max height. Auto. Max speed. The car shot straight up, missed a passing chopterbus by inches, seemed to shudder in air, and hurtled ahead.

Three kilometers later, just under a minute later, he seized control and gasped as he dropped the bottom out of it. The car plummeted. Its screen showed a cluster of cars; he juiced it and joined them. Swerved east and rushed on, beamless, for thirty harrying seconds, swerved west, caught a beam, remained on it for another half-minute, buttoned again and dropped to hirise level.

His pale face began to resume its normal color. The lines, the almost-white spots at the corners of his mouth ebbed away. His breathing slowed and his grim expression relaxed as he tooled the car in the general direction—circuitously—of the interplanetary terminal.

I'm still Wesley Harmon, Licensed Pimp, 727-44-7088. And he said it aloud, to convince himself it was true.

But he knew otherwise. He was something else. He was the essence of a chain of humanity that stretched back over four hundred thousand years. Yes, *humanity*. Some genetic micropart of him remembered with monstrous, incredible clarity.

But what was the rest of it?

"Damned if I know," he muttered, Wesley Harmon, 727-44-7088.

That titanic intrusion of total recall, of recall after four hundred thousand years, had blasted him from the mainstream of consciousness like that last resounding trumpet of Judgment Day. (*Judgment Day? I've seen it, thanks. I was in attendance.*)

The door of time was opening gradually, creakily, with agonizing slowness and yet a speed that was torturous, mind-staggering—and his mind was indeed staggering. But the door was opening. Once through, he could never return to what he had been. Through the haze of remembrance/unremembrance (amnesia?) he groped out for the answer.

The Star Pearls. From . . .

"Mars. Out there—out there is where it began. All of it."

(*where what began?*)

He shook the confusion from his mind and concentrated on threading his way among the city's hirises.

II: BEGINNING OF THE END

The evolutionary process had accelerated with each generation, just as the Survivor had been advised it would. They became . . . people.

On a warm and misty morning, in a far-off glen of the great valley of the Beginning, a female stepped from her hut and watched the males depart on the day's business of hunting. They carried spears. They wore knives—crude or no, knives.

She gazed into the hazy distance where lay the sacred garden, and she frowned in puzzlement, fingers caressing the soft and almost invisible down on her cheek. She remembered something—and yet she could not remember it. She frowned, hesitating, chewing her lower lip.

Then she ducked back through the low doorway of the hut. She moved swiftly. Leather thongs secured a few clay pots together; animal skin formed the pack for dried meat. She peered cautiously through the doorway before moving quickly from the hut and into the jungle.

None saw her leave. But none would have worried overmuch if they had done. She was a silly thing. Only a young female, and she put on airs, her and her straight back and nearly hairless face.

For days she moved through the jungle, avoiding the other villages, escaping the animals that now respected the new kings, who lengthened their arms with the branches of trees. Had she entered a village, she might have been captured and forcibly mated, and she would never learn what she must. She was never attacked by any of the carnivores; this she took as a miraculous sign. Her journey was favored by God. When her store of dried animal flesh was exhausted, she ate the herbs and plants with which she was familiar, cooking them in her clay vessels over small fires in jungle clearings—until the pots were all broken. Still she existed and subsisted, eating raw those berries and plants of which she was sure. Each night she located a climbable tree; each morning she clambered down and moved on, eating as she went, knowing the loneliness of a lost soul.

With feminine determination she thrust on, never questioning the existence of the garden of God, or the logic of her quest. And late one afternoon she stepped from the trees to gaze up at a towering cliff. The seemingly impassable obstacle crushed her, resulting in her first feeling of dismay.

In panic, she wondered if God had placed it there to stop curious mortals such as she. She expected thunderbolts, and worse, momentarily.

They did not come.

Then she saw the old altars at the rock-strewn base of the precipice, and she saw the narrow slash that tore into one side of the barrier. She moved forward. One person. And only a woman. Alone.

Hours later, she was forcing herself to continue her toiling up the path. Her heart pounded within her breast, screaming at her that she was nearing the end of her quest. She heard no sound save the sighing of the wind in the narrow passageway that led higher, ever higher. She was certain that it came from the breath of God, that it led to the garden of Heaven.

She panted with exhaustion and her steps became slower and slower, but in the distance she could hear the sound of a waterfall. The path ended abruptly. She clutched the trunk of a twisting tree for support, almost fainting at the vista before her. This, beyond doubt, was the Garden. Her eyes hoarded its beauty. Not far away was a magnificent castle; beyond that was a shining tower covered with twining vines.

And then he came, stepping through the doorway of the castle.

No: and then He came, and she sank to her knees, for This was God. She was sure of it. No male in the valley possessed such beauty. His golden hair fell to his shoulders, and his naked, muscular body was hairless, gleaming bronze in the sunlight, and his forehead was broad and high.

She was filled with quaking fear when he looked up and saw her. She heard him call out.

"Welcome . . . to heaven."

"Oh my God, forgive me!" She fell forward onto the ground, prostrating herself, trembling in fear. "I have sinned and profaned the sacred Garden!"

The Survivor laughed. "It doesn't appear as if you've profaned anything."

He gazed at her across the musically rippling stream that separated them, and he noticed that she was different from the others. An evolutionary advance! Human-looking. *Pretty!*—even though she was completely covered with a faint down of soft fur.

"Make yourself at home. It gets rather lonely up here."

She rose to her knees and stared at him in awe. "My . . . lord. Are you really God?"

The Survivor smiled. "That all depends on how you look at it. I'm he whom the people of the valley call God, yes. Had they lived as long as I, they would have different thoughts." He strolled over to the bridge that spanned the

69

little stream. He crossed. He approached her, and he sat down on the ground near her. "You'll get a stiff neck if you keep looking up at me. Where did you learn the Old Words? Nobody speaks them any more."

"I—I listened to the shamans," she said. Her fear was dissipating, like fog in the sunlight, as she realized he was not angry with her. "They are so . . . so beautiful, and right. I remembered every one of them."

The Survivor shook his head. "The shaman-priests make a mess of the Old Words. They always distort the syntax and spoil the pronunciation. You speak them almost as well as I. Do you remember . . . anything?"

"Oh, I *do* remember!" The girl was suddenly very earnest. "But—I do not remember what it is I remember. I was standing in front of my father's hut, and suddenly I knew that I had to go and find the place where God lives." She shook her head in bewilderment. "I don't know why."

"I guess it will be that way forever," the Survivor sighed. "It was one of the chances of all this. They'll always search."

They were silent for a few moments; he looked over his small domain. Wearying at last of living in the rocket, he had built a one-room house. Then, one by one, he had added other rooms. Revisions and corrections followed in the illogical progression as he settled down to long-range planning. The second floor and the walls around the artificial pool, slowly; he had a thousand years ahead of him, and there was no reason to hurry. Then the landscaping of the canyon; it occupied hands and mind. The entire transformation had taken nearly a hundred years. But it was better than going insane from the loneliness.

"When did you create us, my lord?" Her voice was tiny, her eyes huge.

"Hm?" The Survivor was jerked back from his mental meanderings, "Oh, I guess that was about two hundred years ago. Something like that, maybe a little more. It wasn't really a creation, but you wouldn't understand that, I'm afraid," He smiled. "You wouldn't understand the truth if I told you, detail by detail."

"It—was not—really a . . . creation?" The girl was horrified.

He merely smiled. "No."

"Then . . . you are not really . . . God?"

He smiled.

EIGHT...

The blowup at the planetarium had placed Wes in a precarious position. By now his description was being distributed throughout the city. But at least they didn't have his name—and he hoped no one had recorded his license number. In the suburbs, he dropped down to a branch of his bank. He waited, almost without breathing, for the one car ahead of him to get its business transacted. Then he pulled forward into the rooftop booth.

A pretty brunette smiled at him on the screen, said something pleasant, and opened the tray. He dropped in his card, and a moment later watched her scan it quickly. She inserted it into the credifier on her desk, waited the few necessary seconds for the machine to tell her the card was authentic and that its owner rated eight on a credscale of ten. She gave him her best bank smile.

"I'm taking a business trip to Europe. I'll need ten thousand in interplanetary cred coupons." He smiled and added, "I may find I have to leave Earth when I get there, and I'd rather handle it here."

"Of course," she said, her little frown vanishing.

"Would you also please contact the Bank of Urbanova and guarantee thirty thousand. Authority granted to set it aside," he said, knowing she was recording.

"Of course," she said again, smiling and doing things with her fingers to buttons on the console before her.

"We can laser the call and have the word there far before you, even if you were leaving right now."

"Please do. Charge the call to my account."

A few more seconds, and the slot above the drive-in tray began regurgitating books of cred coupons. He pocketed them, nodded his thanks, and started away.

"I hope you enjoy your trip, Harmon," she said.

Yeah, he thought, flashing a smile back at her as he buttoned the car up and away from the bank. Well, he'd accomplished that. He'd tried to throw them off by saying he was heading for Europe, but if he hadn't indicated the possibility of Mars there'd just have been a confab while he explained why he wanted IP coupons. He doubted he'd thrown anyone off much if they decided he was dangerous enough to pursue to Mars—or, like the bank, beam up a description of him.

So he wouldn't be able to take passage, then. He'd have to get there some other way. He was both a hunting man and a hunted one, now. A streak jerked his head to the right, and he watched a big Marsliner jump upward.

I'll bet she and her partner are on that ship, he thought, but he twitched his shoulders in a shrug. *I'll find them. I'll follow them right out into the asteroids, if necessary.*

Odd thought; what put that into my mind? The asteroids, for godsake!

But there was no doubt in his mind that the actions of the two he pursued were inextricably woven into the fabric of his past. And, obviously, his future.

He flashed past the sprawling spaceport and on into the open country until he neared a line of cheapjack stores and cafés. Spacehand City, they called it. Fights every night, killings with ugly regularity.

He didn't lock the car. He'd probably never see it again.

He moved easily along the immobile pedway—sidewalk, they used to be called—worming his way through the extraordinarily motley crowd without shoving. This was Wildcat Row, and there were many more of them on the three planets. It was as shoddy and dangerous as it looked, but it was no place for tramps—unless the wildcat couriers could be considered such. Rough, independent to the

73

point of meanness, these were the gun-toting men who carried freight that was too small for the great liners . . . or too questionable. In their turn they offered what the big companies and Gov carriers could not: lack of curiosity and the small-craft ability to set down anywhere. Their services were available to anyone who had the price, which was never cheap. They were as indispensable as they were disreputable. Planetary authorities discreetly ignored them and the fact that the wildcatters obstinately refused to register their ships on any planet.

Wes Harmon was a big man, and he had no hesitation about mingling with these people, but he avoided shoving, just the same. He ambled into Eddie's, his eyes flicking over the patrons as he headed for the bar. His clothing drew glances; his size and eyes reduced any comment to whispers. Leaning on the bar, he caught the eye of the man behind it. He doubletook, grinned, and headed his way.

"How the drill are you, Wes? What the vut you doing down here?"

Wes slapped the outstretched hand. "Slumming, what else?" he said with a grin. He leaned one elbow on the bar and half turned to survey the dark room. "Not much like your old place, Eddie."

"Edward's Fashion Lounge? Bullshit! Going bankrupt's no fun. Those geedee sponsored brats ruined me, Wes; whaddaya think of that? Gov lets the fatcats sponsor a kid so they'll have somebody to leave their fortune to, and as soon's the kids are big enough they start coming in, running up a tab. Daddy doesn't know about it and when he finds out he doesn't like it, and guess what happens when he takes it to court?"

"Eddie's," Wes said. "But that only happened to you once, jacko."

"Yeah." Eddie sighed. "But it sounds so much better than admitting I'm a stupid bug." He glanced around with an air of contentment. "Anyway, I get a better deal here. Too much competition down on the main drag, and the overhead was murder. These characters aren't fancy, but they *spend*. Sure, they spend the big bulk in town, but I

74

get first and last crack at it. Crewmen make as much as twenty thou on an IP run, and I bet my shirt there's not a jacko here on speaking terms with a bank. The skippers save, but only to keep their ships running. We—" Eddie broke off, turned his eyes on Wes. "You're on the air, you know."

"Good description?" Wes took out a cigaret.

"Electronic mockup. Fair, but not perfect." Eddie turned his head. "Yeah yeah, be there in a min—*Lucy*! HELP!" To Wes, "They don't know who you are, and they probably won't find out if you don't put on another show or make an exhibit of that pretty face. Car outside? *That* they described good."

"Just down the street." Wes tossed the keys on the counter. "It's yours. Repaint it and have fun."

"Min." Eddie moved down the bar, bent to whisper at the huge fat man there, slid the keys across into his hand. The ape left swiftly. Eddie returned to Harmon.

"It don't make sense, Wes," he said, opening a pottle of Wiedemann's, Earth's Oldest Beer, and setting it before Harmon. "That was a wild story they 'cast, jacko. You really do that?"

Wes shrugged. "Ask me no questions, Eddie. But I'm up to my eyeballs in something you'd never believe. You remember Lorna?"

"I sure do!" Eddie's smile flashed on again and he wiggled his brows. "A real gorgeous heff—something for the *big* man."

"Not any more, Eddie. Some mental misfits fixed her so you'd never recognize her—if you could stand to look at her."

"Oh god no, Wes! Not that sweet—ah." He nodded slowly. "I see. No wonder you fobbed out. And now you're out to cream the bastards?"

"Pos." Wes jerked a thumb back toward the IP terminal. "I think they just left on the Marsliner. I can't wait a couple of weeks for the next ship, Eddie. I won't."

Eddie nodded, looking dolorous. "Sorry, Wes. You *know* these couriers won't take passengers, for any amount of money."

Wes tapped the thick sheaf of interplanetary cred coupons on the counter. "Here's any amount of money. Will a crewman give up his berth, Eddie?"

"Hmm! Interesting thought. I don't know." His eyes searched about the room. "Wait a min. No promises, but—" He sauntered down to the other end of the bar where there was a man wearing an old-fashioned burr-cut and what was obviously a made-on-Mars jac. Wes watched them talk, watched the man's eyes study him. Eddie turned, motioned.

As Wes approached the two men, two others rose from a little table just behind them and, along with two strictly lowgrade j-girls, departed. Wes sat quickly at the table.

"Join me, gents," he said, with a little smile, and Eddie and his friend moved to the table.

"Wes, meet Isaac Vanipoor. Izzy, Wes Harmon."

Wes surveyed the other man: thick and broad-shouldered, the black burr starting well back above his rising forehead. Izzy's hand came out. When Harmon started to tap it, it closed—and squeezed. *One of those. Big boy wants to play big man.* Wes squeezed back, with no outward sign of effort.

"I give up," Izzy said at last. "Release the remnants." He flexed his fingers, studying them. Then he made his scrutiny of Harmon's clothing obvious. "You look fancy, but you've got muscle you haven't used yet, and Eddie says you can space. Prove that?"

Wes found the card and handed it over. Izzy made an impressed face.

"Four-star rating. Be damned. You can't beat that." Shaking his head, he handed it back and sipped his coffee. He glanced at Eddie, at Wes, and shrugged.

"I've got a berth on a sealed cargo shipment for Mars. I don't know what it is, and I don't care. I can make ten thou on the trip. I might not get another like it for as long as two weeks. What've you got to make it worth my while to wait?"

Wes told him without hesitation. "Five thou."

"Let's see the cred, fred."

"This do?" Wes counted out five coupon booklets. The

76

spaceman picked them up, riffled the pages, and pursed his lips in a soundless whistle.

"Gov seal," Eddie pointed out.

"Instant conversion," Wes said. "Needs my signature, that's all."

Izzy glanced around, hunching over the books. "Jesus, jacko, you gotta be crazy coming down here with all this! Just one little problem, though——"

"I'll cash 'em, Iz," Eddie said.

Izzy looked at him, back at Wes, and smiled slowly. He returned the books.

"So sign 'em, friend, plus another five hun; there'll be a small payoff. Records, you know. Mind flying with a homie?"

"Only if he bites it off," Wes said, signing, slapping his credcard down on the face of each book, signing, slapping . . .

NINE...

The big spacer trudged down the narrow road to the
bunkers, gear bag slung over his shoulder and bumping
his broad back. His clothes looked new, but inexpensive.
Not unlike many others on their way Out, he paused and
turned to look back.

In the distance beyond Wildcat Row and Spacehand
City, the great League capitol rose into the night sky,
dimming the stars with glowing, flickering light. Tubeways
curled among the towering buildings like delicate cobwebs,
carelessly strung. Somewhere on the other side of the
city, on the twentieth floor of a soaring hirise, several
superlatively handsome young women were about to adjust
to the fact that their pimp brother was no longer there.

Wes shifted the gearbag and glanced up at the sky.
"Adios, past."

It was something that happened to others, if it happened. A brief interval of improbable events, suddenly
combining to slam havoc into a man's life and restore
to his mind ghastly memories (that should have died with
the collision, time out of mind, of two planets). Wesley
Harmon had heard of the course of a man's life being
altered in a moment. He hadn't believed it. Or if he had,
he had assumed, naturally, that he was immune. But fate's
hammer was an irresistible force. He, too, had fallen under
its blow.

He shook the thoughts from his mind and turned to walk on down the road. *Adios, Earth.*

Unlike the great terminal only a few miles distant, the wildcat field was comparatively quiet. A small courier ship, roaring up the chute and being hurled off into an orbit that would spiral and spiral until it was slingshot out into space, drew hardly a glance. Wes watched it, though until he reached the bunker with the big 43 on it.

Close up, the couriercraft loomed large; it was small only by comparison to the liners. A third of it housed the powerful engines; about two percent was given over to living quarters—just enough to keep a man from fobbing out on the long trip—and the remaining bulk was for payload. The number on the side of the ship was 4537, the name along the space-weathered hull MISS SCOTTY.

Light streamed from an open airlock and Wes looked up at the unrecognizable face and short body of a man. "Harmon?"

"Right. Manuel Schultheis?"

"Right. Come up."

Wes tried not to grin. Some strange combination of names emerged from the government creches; this one was a real deuce. "Had to buy some stuff on the Row. Sorry I'm late."

Manny laughed. "You must be reeeal new, jacko! Nobody's late in this racket. We don't punch clocks for NObody." He stepped back as Wes reached the top of the ramp.

The two men exchanged scrutinies. Manuel was stocky, shortish, with a great deal of wavy brown hair on his massive head. His color was fairer than Harmon's; more time in space than in Earth's sunlight, maybe.

"Manny," he said. "Anybody gets formal on this ship gets his tailbone kicked out into space, Wes. Iz said you're four-star. Whee—that's more'n that drunken space-jockey is. Ever pilot one of these?"

Wes lowered his bag to the deck. "Nope. I got that rating mastering a yacht between here and Luna. This looks like a slice of cake."

Buttoning the airlock-close, Manny ripped out a quick

Mars-type oath and grabbed the manual lever. He looked at Wes with brows up.

"*Yacht!*" He shook his head, laughing. "You'll have no problem with this fireball, then. And don't worry about me wondering why you're not piloting that thing any more, either. I don't wonder about *anything*. It's a good way to live, just tending your own little store. All I need's an extra man to spell me at the con and engine room and handle the cargo."

"You've got him."

Manny nodded and led the way. He gestured at an oval hatchway. "Toss your gear into a locker and come on into the con cabin."

Wes did.

"Sit down quick," Manny told him as he stepped into the instrument-filled con. "We're about to be berthed."

Wes gave him a look. "You planning on staying in the co-seat?"

"Yes, sir, jacko, I can't think of a better way to check out those quadrupe stars of yours than to watch you space us. Oops—here goes. Buckle up, peelot." He watched Wes drop quickly into the seat and whip the straps across himself; the ship was moving. Harmon studied the console and gauges before him as the little port's dated equipment transferred them to a chute.

"You're berthed and cleared, four-five-three-seven."

"You're read," Manny snapped back. "Keep everybody happy till I get back, Sam."

"Find a meteorite," Tower said, and Manny grinned and nodded to Wes and Wes moved them out.

Up and around and out, hurled into space with cheekbones biting skin and heart massaging backbone and hands covered with skin made of lead. Around and around, faster and faster, and around—and Wes watched the dials and the screens and goosed, and Miss Scotty was sent hurtling out into space like a rock from David's sling.

"Nice," Manny said. "Nice, Wes. Set her on auto-acceleration while I check the cargo. I didn't hear a thing, though."

Wes went to work. Days would pass before they reached

the velocity that would get them to Mars soonest, but he pushed it, thinking as computerly as possible while he adjusted the instruments and triple-checked all of it. Then he went back to find Manny geigering the crates in the hold.

"Anything wrong?"

"Negative. I always doublecheck these sealed cargoes just to be on the safe side. Somebody ships something hot, I can't take chances with leakage. This hold isn't sealed like the engine room." He jerked his head back to his counter as it chittered. "Uh-huh. Somebody's sending some radioactives. Just warm, though." He jerked his head. "Drag that silver tarp over here, Wes. It's lined with radiation blockers."

Working together, they covered the crates until Manny was satisfied they were totally shielded.

The two men spent several days—by the ship's chronometer—checking out the vessel preparatory to locking it on Auto for the duration of the run. Manny was impressed with his partner's plotting, and he was big enough to say so. Eventually the ship was running itself, and it would continue until someone told it otherwise.

"Not like the luxury liners," Manny said. "Those ships have everything you can think of to keep people busy on the long run—even swimpools, for godsake. I used to read a lot, and I tried everything from autochess to plain and fancy drinking. But both hooch and books take up space, and space is what we're selling. Microfilm reprints'll never replace turning pages, not to this jacko."

Wes nodded. He knew the feeling.

"Past few years, Wes, I've taken up collecting pornofilm. There's a lot of good specialty stuff being put out these days."

Wes smiled, wondering what the shorter man would think if he were told his aide was a financially successful pimp. "Got some good ones?"

From where he lay on his bunk, Manny jerked his head "up" at a mounted cabinet. "That box's holding some of the hottest stuff ever put on film. It's expensive, buying the

81

best color-definition jobs on microspools, but—hell! If you can't collect the best, why bother?"

He stretched against his webbing to open the cabinet.

Shortly after, Wes was watching the wildest scene he'd witnessed since that new-rich Marser had hired every girl on the premises and coked himself up on SuprLibid.

And shortly after that, Wes was learning that Manny was without doubt peerless as a homie. It did tend to shorten the trip. Lack of reciprocity did not disturb him one bit, fortunately.

Harmon listened to the clump-clump sounds and the whooshes from the airlock. He turned on the amplifier, then had to turn it quickly down when Manny's voice blared at him.

"Receive me loud and clear?"

"Clear and too vutting loud, Manny. How's the view out there?"

"Absolutely beautiful. Great night for a walk."

"What d'you see? We haven't picked up a satellite or two have we?"

"Must've been a loner. I don't even see a new mark. I'm going to check out the stern. Safety line's attached— don't think you're going to lose me."

Wes chuckled and waited, listening to Manny's breathing. He'd kidded him yesterday; keep eating the way you do and we'll have to adust for your new weight before we can get this thing down on Mars. And now this strange impact on the hull . . . .

"Hey, I found it, Wes. Nothing much. Little dent, about twelve inches long by an inch or so at the center. Whatever it was almost missed us."

"Shouldn't give us any trouble in planetfall." Wes shrugged. "That's no more than a scratch. Come on home and I'll consider selling you Boardwalk."

"Liar! We've been playing that same game for something like five Earthdays, and you haven't given me a break yet. Listen, punch this in, Wes. I'm measuring. Atmospheric friction could deepen this thing as we come in. It's about fifteen meters back from—"

Manny's voice shot up the scale in a scream of agony, then became a bubbling sound.

"Manny! WHAT HAPPENED?"

searing torture of crushed bones and riven flesh that filled his universe in a monstrous moment before ruptured arteries streamed crimson floods out through the ripped suit

"Manny! What—"

"I'm—dead man, Wes. Half . . . of me . . . crushed." His voice was weak; it went lower. "Stay . . . put, jacko. Letting—air out of helmet . . . suit . . . I don't even know . . . where it came . . . cut me loose . . . don't drag a . . . corpse. Record: this . . . ship and cargo are . . . Wesley Harmon's . . . ."

pain red scarlet black awful searing tearing guts spewing god Earth poor Manny poor little can't do it got to . . . THERE!

Wes found him on the viewer. Manny was—had been —right. He was squashed, jellied. It had to be what Wes had suggested—they'd picked up a parasite, a satellite. It had come around again and smashed the man—or it had had a partner. It was done with now; Manny had not just released the air, he'd opened his faceplate. Wes squeezed his eyes shut. Blindly, he shut off the screen.

He waited an hour, then another. Nothing else. If they'd found the swarm everyone had used to laugh at when the movies showed them, they were out of it. If they'd proved that one chance in a trillion trillion doesn't mean impossible-never, that chunk of rock or iron was long gone. And so was Manny.

Wes dragged himself to the locker, suited up, entered the airlock, and stared at the outer door. He released the air, counted ten, and opened the outer lock. With extreme care he reached outside. Yes. Manny had done it all according to the book. His line was clamped on the very first ring. Himself tethered to the inner airlock door, Wes fished out his utility knife and waited and waited for his hand to come up. Snuggling his fist in against the hull so that the knife was pointed outward into space, he set it against Manny's line. And pushed the stud up. No sound, *no feeling* as the laser beam sliced through the line. But it had, and the line was gone. Manny was gone.

Covered with sweat and unable to control his shivering, Wes Harmon had to talk to himself: to be certain that he was inside, that he closed the outer door, that he made certain it was dogged, that he voided the airlock, that he pumped air into it. Then he opened the inner door and re-entered the ship.

Hours later, he was still spacesuited, floating aimlessly in the silent ship, wondering.

Was he some sort of curse? How many people would this happen to? How many would touch his life with theirs—and die horribly? How many could *he* stand? (How many times had it happened, in the past? He did not know. He remembered only part of the beginning: the end, and the beginning of the beginning: the flight from cataclysm. The landing on the primitive planet. The aloneness. The only human in the universe.)

And through it all, creeping about in his mind on dark legs, the thought that he was not whole, that he had lost something, forever.

Still later, remembering at last to strip out of the sweatstenchy suit, he drew out the little box. He stared at it. The Star Pearl. How did it fit in? How did any of it fit together? (Not chance. Chance hadn't sent him to that planetarium. Chance hadn't sent the rock that had killed Manny. Chance had not placed him here, alone in the middle of nothing, with only his brain—*his* brain?—for company.) He had to find those people, because of what they'd done to Lorna. She was his sister (wasn't she? Did he—had he had another sister? Perhaps long ago—). Why was something so important to that grisly couple that they had had to torture that completely innocent girl—

(*distance is only the measure of the movement of an object through time*)

—that they'd had to resort to such a monstrous act? He was certain that they also held the key to another time—

84

(time is only the measure of the movement of an object through space)

Lorna.

Another time.

(before Ur of the Chaldees crept from the mud of the Euphrates)

Lorna heard the voices and floated up from the comforting womb of unconsciousness. She felt the vague aching in her body, and she remembered, and she began to moan, softly. "Don't burn me again! Don't hurt me. Please don't hurt me . . ."

TEN...

"Don't hurt me . . ."

One of the physicians gazed at her with more than clinical interest. "This is a perplexing problem, Doctor. We've had her through regeneration twice, and she's already beginning to change. That's still a badly scarred body, but the machine had limits . . . it can only utilize available cellular material."

"It's much better than what the ancients were able to do with their steel knives, Doctor!"

"Um. But look at these holophotos. Look at her features, her body. She'd never be able to live with a body like that, much less this—face." He drew a deep, slow breath. "It'd drive her out of her mind. We don't want to lose what we've already salvaged, Doctor. I say take her as far back as necessary, and use the metabolic rectificator, too."

A raised eyebrow. "That will draw on a lot of tissue supply, Ben. It can't help but result in physical regression. Does the contract protect us against responsibility for psychological disorientation?"

"It does. We're safe. Form 25-A; complete release."

"Another ten cc's, nurse."

Barely able to feel the injection of Psychotran, Lorna slid softly back into sleep.

It seemed that only a moment passed before she opened

her eyes and raised a hand to rub the sleep from them. She looked around, blinking.

"Wes?" She frowned. "Hey—where am I?"

She gasped; the voice of a little girl was echoing her words. She glanced about; saw no one. "Who are you?" Again the echo. Lorna felt a sudden twinge of alarm. "WHERE ARE YOU/WHERE ARE YOU?"

Slowly, carefully, staring at the opposite wall, she touched her lips. The voice had come from her! —And then she remembered, and she sat there and shook, violently, for long minutes.

This time her hand rose fearfully to touch her face; the face she knew must be a ghastly travesty. Her fingers touched soft, smooth flesh. She found a slight chubbiness under her chin, in the cheeks. She gasped. Hurling aside the covers, she stared down at herself.

"Good god, it can't BE!"

She swung her legs out of the bed to the floor—and stumbled back against the bed; the floor was further than it should have been. Regaining her balance, she saw the mirror. Her bare feet padded softly as she went to it. And stared.

The girl in the mirror stared back at her with an ingenuous expression of astonishment. She was cute, young, perhaps in her teens, perhaps not quite. The delicate little nose surmounted cherubic lips that were years away from maturity. She gasped at sight of the small, conical breasts, the obviously adolescent figure below. Her chin started to tremble. She swallowed a tightness in her throat. It didn't go down.

Then she glanced over her shoulder as the door opened.

The nurse was blond, tall, flattish at the top, slim but overbroad in the hips. She had a nice smile, though. "Good morning, Lorna. I'm sorry I wasn't here when you woke up, honey. I could have made it easier."

Lorna glanced back at the mirror, then turned her dismayed face on the nurse. "Is—is it really . . . me?"

"The nurse set her tray on the little table and regarded the nude girl with concern. She'd be throwing screaming fobbies, if it weren't for the load of Psychotran they'd pumped her full of. The nurse's smile was carefully, professionally cheerful. "You look just like a normal fourteen-year-old girl, honey. Just about that, anyhow. You'll get used to it. It was the only way it could be done." She chuckled. "Look on the bright side: you're a virgin again."

"Oh, wow." The high-pitched little voice was irritating; Lorna couldn't forget the years she'd spent developing her throaty sexiness. And her bosom . . . all those hormones! "How'm I supposed to be a practicing jay-girl with a sweet li'l voice like this? And this bod—and I'm even shorter! My regulars wouldn't even *recognize* me."

"Why not eat your breakfast and stop worrying, hm? My name's Evelyn, by the way." She pushed a chair up to the table, and her expression went serious. "Really, Lorna. It couldn't have been corrected any other way. No one's ever been brought in here the way you were, alive or otherwise. They've done an unbelievable job. There isn't a spat of scar tissue on you. The choice was to leave you at chronological age twenty-seven and scarred for life, or this. Permitting a physical regression to adolescence, using every scrap of available tissue and a lot that wasn't, really. It worked out, Lorna. You have a lovely little form."

Lorna pouted. "Little's right! I look like a daisy-fresh crecheling. I've a good mind to throw a crecheling-size tantrum."

Evelyn gave her a steady-eyed stare. "You throw *any* kind of tantrum, darling, and I swear I'll paddle your tail till it's red as your hair. Now sit down and eat your breakfast, young lady."

The adult command jerked at her mind. Her body started to move automatically. No, no, she was Lorna, she was twenty-seven, she didn't have to—but—

She trotted obediently over to the table and sat down to eat.

The nurse smiled, nodded, patted the girlish shoulder. "Don't rush yourself, baby. I'll be back in about an hour. Eat first, then think."

She stepped out of the room and listened to the latch click before she went down the hall to her station. She

Come for the filter...

A PRODUCT OF
Lorillard

KENT
WITH
THE FAMOUS MICRONITE FILTER

DELUXE LENGTH

18 mg. "tar," 1.2 mg. nicotine av. per cigarette, FTC Report Oct. '74.

...you'll stay for the taste.

DELUXE LENGTH

KENT
WITH
THE FAMOUS MICRONITE FILTER

A lot of good taste that comes easy through the Micronite filter.

18 mg. "tar," 1.2 mg. nicotine av. per cigarette, FTC Report Oct. '74.

Warning: The Surgeon General Has Determined That Cigarette Smoking Is Dangerous to Your Health.

buttoned Doctor Eversole and waited. The screen lit and he smiled at her.

"Well Evelyn, how'd she take it?"

"Weren't you watching?"

He shook his head. "Negative. I'll rely on you for reports. I don't want to interfere or contact her until she's stabilized. Only a woman can handle that part. Is she accepting it?"

Evelyn shrugged with a pale smile. "She's loaded with Psychotran V-3; she hasn't any choice. Of course she's accepting it. Her emotional reactions are strictly adolescent, and she can't suppress them. I'm treating her like a child, but it still seems weird, knowing her background. Are you sure you want her to progress in that direction?"

"It's the only possible course," he told her, nodding.

"The only alternative would be to risk dissociation, even schizophrenia. Don't worry about it. We have a carte-blanche contract. Just report regularly and don't let her out of that room until she's stabilized."

He blanked the screen. Evelyn hesitated a moment, then screened the girl's room.

Lorna ate in staring-eyed silence. Unaware of the Ps-V-3 in her system, she was bewildered by the mental block; it allowed no serious concern about the events that led to her present condition. The knowledge was there, but it slid elusively away from her mental fingers. And she was hungry.

When she'd emptied the tray, she wandered about the room, adjusting herself to a four-walled environment. And glancing, again and again, at the mirror. She had to compensate for her new size; everything was a little higher than she—remembered? She found the newest antique rage, movie magazines, atop the dresser, and she carried them over to curl up in the armchair. She was not aware of any strangeness in her wide-eyed fascination with the male sex stars, with the pictorialization and descriptions of scenes. Her breathing quickened.

Suddenly she threw down the magazine and pressed her hands to her cheeks. She felt the heat, knew she was blushing furiously. "What am I *doing*? An experienced joygirl getting all flashy over a simple pornozine!"

Only a moment later, the door opened and the nurse entered with an armload of clothing. "Here's your new wardrobe, dear—hey! What's got you so . . ." She gazed down at the magazine, up at Lorna's face. "Oh, poor baby. Is that all it took? Your background's getting mixed up with your foreground." She dumped the clothes on the dresser.

Lorna was too astonished at her own reaction to reply immediately. A wise smile curved Evelyn's lips, but Lorna mind was a whirl of confusion as she stared up at the blonde.

"Well," Evelyn said quietly, "there's no sense in wasting all this. This is an area where I can definitely be of help."

Lorna waited, trembling. She had a fleeting thought that this wasn't quite right. She should know what to do, but her body and her emotional reactions were those of an adolescent. But the nurse was very nice, and it worked out just beautifully. The relaxing therapy was far older than Phychotran, even than Ur of the Chaldees.

"Director Blake of Guild Protector Service is here, Doctor."

"Send him in." He turned back to the big console, keyed in a question on screen three, and adjusted a dial until the light turned amber again. He did not glance up when the door opened. "Sit down, Blake. Through in a minute."

Blake dropped into the comfortable chair facing the desk, resting his briefcase on its edge. "Still playing the piano, George?"

Eversole nodded. "Permanent occupation. But it's better than what they had to contend with in the old days." Of the twelve separate control panels and screens on the console, five were active. He checked them carefully against the electronic progress charts, keyed in questions, made adjustments that would add or substract, increase or decrease this or that medication or treatment to the patient represented by the screen. Making a final adjustment, he flexed his fingers, turned, and palmed a jade relaxer. "I haven't seen you since you brought in Harmon's jay."

"How is she, George?"

"Haven't you been getting the reports?"

Blake sighed. "Yeah, I scanned them. Was it totally necessary to regress her so far?"

George leaned forward and clasped his hands. "Positive. The only alternative was a scarred body and an incurable mental case. You saw her; that wasn't just epidermal damage. She was a . . . mess." He held up a hand as Blake opened his mouth. "I know what you're going to say. The girls in the felinism houses come out looking fresh as a daisy. But that isn't real torture, Ike. It's sexo-maso stimulation, felinism, and they know when to stop. The person who worked this girl over did the job with the deliberate attempt to create . . . horror."

"Deliberate? You don't think it was a maniac?"

The doctor shook his head. "Can't. Oh, maybe, but it was done with a purpose, almost scientifically. He *drew lines* on her with that . . . whatever it was. Systematically." He tapped the relaxer against the desktop, frowning. "There's still a puzzle, though. The actual wounds were somewhat ragged, shaky, as though they *were* made by a lunatic. As though . . . as though there were two people involved, a maniac following orders. Which is impossible. Anyone that far gone would be completely oblivious to instructions. Well, that's not my department." He leaned back in his chair, fingering the smoothness of the relaxer. "What was the effect on Harmon?"

"Where've you been? Don't you ever watch the news?"

"Not often, Ike, too many other things to do. You should see the backlog of eduscanning I've got taped. Why? Was there something about this?"

"When Harmon left me that night, George, he was out to kill somebody." Blake spread his hands. "You can't blame him for that. A few hours later, there was an alert: the description fitted him. He'd gone berserk and shot up the Metropolitan Planetarium. Since then he's vanished.

Well, not really; I think he's gone off to Mars. But not by standard means."

The doctor raised his brows. "Sounds bad—that was over a month ago. He'll be a job for psycho-conditioning when they find him."

"If they do, yes. It's a damned shame." Pulling out one of his black nobac cigars, Blake fiddled with it. "He was —I mean, is—one of the good guys. Took good care of his girls." He fired up the cigar. "And now if he doesn't surface within six months I'm going to have him crossed off as dead. Guild insurance covers that girl, by the way, completely."

"Uh, what about the other girls? Did you get them a new proc?"

Blake nodded, pluming smoke and studying the cigar. "Just temporary—for now. Placement ran off a psycho-pattern check and found a man the girls should adjust to easily. Surprisingly close facsimile of Harmon." He chuckled. "Would you believe it—the new pimp's Japanese."

Eversole grinned. "Interesting, but I'm not amazed. Recurring psychopatterns aren't unusual. Most of us seem to've come out of pretty much the same mold, originally. Well, now you people are left with the problem of Lorna. I've had to assign her an arbitrary age of about sixteen. Because of the psycho-physical problems involved, her memories will eventually submerge into her subconscious to a point where she may not even be able to retrieve them. She won't lose her identity, but she'll be living a new life. That's your problem." The doctor leaned forward. "She can't go back to being a joygirl. So far as her present condition is concerned, she's too *young* to license."

Blake was nodding. "Working on it. Legal staff's preparing credentials identifying her as a Sponsored Juvenile."

"Forged?"

Blake cleared his throat and looked away, then swung his head back with a smile. "We won't be able to assign her to a sponsor, though, until the paperwork's finished. There's still the matter of arranging for . . . adjusting Gov files. *That* will take a while. These things have to be done carefully.

"So carefully I didn't hear a word you said," Eversole assured him.

"Um. I wish I could dispose of the Star Pearl problem so easily."

Eversole looked a question. "What are they, Ike?"

"You don't *know*? Hell, even Gov knows about them!"

Eversole smiled, then spun at a beep sound. He watched a dial and the changing color of a winking light, made an adjustment to the console. The light burned green. "Beautiful," he whispered, and swung back. "Look, Ike, civilization is made up of billions of private lives and hundreds of millions of separate information groups. What's important to one group is totally unknown to others, communications or not. Gov knows about a lot of things because governments are information crossroads. It would be *nice* if we all knew everything, sort of a racial consciousness, but that ain't the way it is. My info group's on a different road—and no, I don't know what the Star Pearls are."

"Remind me not to ask you any more questions," Ike said, making a face. "Better get me something for these ashes, or you'll be sorry." He began explaining while Eversole found a saucer in his desk and passed it across. He listened carefully.

"How did Harmon get mixed up with the things, Ike?"

"Couple of his girls were given Star Pearls by wealthy clients. Both fobbed out; the usual reaction. Everything seemed to go haywire for Harmon. Somebody—unknown—began taking shots at him, and there *may* be a connection between that and the stones. They never hit him, but he started carrying a gun, and finally killed one of them. He was GunTek; guess how much information *they* gave me. You know the rest of it. It drove Wes over the edge; it would anyone, I think."

Eversole rose and walked to the window. After looking out a few seconds, he turned back to Blake. "The whole business sounds irrational, Ike. A simple stone couldn't affect anyone's *mind*. That only—"

He broke off, following Blake's gaze. The Protector was staring at the relaxer on Eversole's desk. Blake grinned at him.

"George, this is a 'simple stone' like Lorna's an 'average' sixteen-year-old. I've just had one analyzed by a gem lab— I was taking it back to the office when I decided to stop off here." He opened his briefcase and set the white box on the desk. Slowly, Eversole came over to open the box.

Resting in a bed of cotton was a largish stone, violet in tone, with a yellowish hint gleaming from its depths. But as he bent closer he saw red, and blue, and that was green . . . "Hm. Prismatic effect. And beautiful, not to mention unusual. Do men ever wear them?"

"No. They're too big, and they can't be split."

"Can't be—it looks so *fragile*!"

Blake snorted. "Fragile, hell! The things seem to be impervious to everything. Of course, nothing heavy's been tried on it. A gem lab isn't equipped for engineering problems. But everything they tried, including the little hammer-and-chisel arrangements they use, just slid off that thing. Without a scratch, as you can see. Finally they put it under the ultra microscope, and then they gave up."

Doctor Eversole sat down and leaned back, frowning. "Why? What'd they find?"

"Nothing." Blake stared petulantly at the jewel. "Get ready, George. They couldn't find that this thing has any molecular structure."

Eversole laughed. Blake didn't. The doctor's frown began before the smile faded. "But that isn't possible!"

"You're right."

"Every solid has a molecular structure—and that jewel's certainly solid." He thumped it with his relaxer. "It's solid enough to this chunk of jade. Suppose—could there be a surface-energy layer of some sort that blocks out electronic probing?"

"We tried that, thanks."

"Then what the vutting hell *is* the thing?"

Blake saw to the conscientious murder of his cigar in the ashtray.

"God knows."

III: BEGINNING OF THE BEGINNING

The girl was horrified. "Then . . . you are not really . . . God?"

The Survivor smiled.

Then he had to laugh. "Don't look so shocked! There may well be a god somewhere, but I don't happen to be it. To be quite truthful, you're the first who's had the intelligence to suspect the truth. Otherwise, you would never have dared come to me." He examined her face carefully, noting the familiar contours, and he sighed. "I think I know why you came. I know who you are, but you're too submerged ever to know who I am."

The girl looked confused for several moments longer, and then her innocent eyes filled with the wonder of what he had said, of his nudeness, and her face brightened. "If you are not God, then you can mate with me!"

The Survivor cocked his head to one side, looking at her in not-quite-astonishment. "The fastest proposition, surely, since sentience!"

As he gazed at her, a sudden tropical shower began to sprinkle from the sky. He jerked his head and wiped at his face. "Young lady, you do not know what you're asking for. My lifespan is a thousand years. I'll be alive long, long after you've . . . gone."

It had been two hundred years since he had touched a woman, and she was almost a woman, enough to be more than attractive. She should be, of course, being who she was! She was beginning to make his pulse race, and he knew he was displaying physical evidence of his arousal as he contemplated whether to hold to the morality of another world, long dead.

When the planets rushed together in mutual destruction, several ships made the escape attempt. Only one succeeded, and came back. There is one human, one Survivor, in the universe. And the load of prisms he (He?) brought: artificially imprinted genetic patterns. I used them to imprint the natives here: reincarnation! And here, before me, is the . . . reincarnation of . . . her. The one person I loved above all on a planet now dead . . . my sister.

No longer awed, she moved closer to him. Her eyes shone.

"A thousand years! Oh, how wonderful! You will remain beautiful all my life." Her hand touched his arm, diffidently. But she was a female, not a male who dare not touch a god. "I can cook for you. I know all the herbs and plants that are good to eat." Her wide eyes searched his face. The fingers of her small hand pressed his arm as she added softly, "I shall fill your house with children."

He tried to control himself, but his arm slipped around her waist and she flowed softly against him. Flowed softly —and pressed hard. He caressed the almost-hardness of her breast, its fur incredibly soft against his palm. Then his lips touched hers, and two centuries of that most unnatural of human states shrieked within him for an end to celibacy. They sank down, and he rolled her easily onto her back, pressing her into the wet grass. The rain poured down over them.

He was quickly reminded that she was little more than a wild animal, but her actions only inflamed him as her wet fur caressed his skin, all over. She squirmed, murmuring in the language of the valley and in the Old Words, mingled with wordless sounds of ecstatic delight.

"My lord! My lord! Fill me with love!"

Her lord did, and by this one act he deepened his godhead, and changed the world, the universe, all universes but one, and eventually, Wesley and Lorna Harmon.

At last they were still once more, lying in contented embrace as their bodies were caressed by the wind and the rain at the beginning of the world.

ELEVEN...

Evelyn entered Lorna's room and walked quickly over to the window to open the curtains before shaking the girl's shoulder. "Come on, honey, wake up."

Lorna opened her eyes and yawned. Both hands came up to rub away the sleep, in the manner of the young girl she resembled. Working her way from under the covers, she sat up on the edge of the bed and scratched. Her hands dropped loosely into her lap as her eyes tried to decide whether to remain open.

"Come on, come on, get yourself a shower and put on your best duds."

Lorna's head snapped up. "What for?"

"After breakfast we're going out on the town. Two weeks is long enough for you to be cooped up in one room."

With a squeaky squeal of delight, Lorna galloped to the bathroom. Evelyn shook her head with a little smile. It was difficult to accept the fact that this was—had been—a twenty-seven-year-old woman with a sensuous, sophisticated personality. But she'd seen the hideously scarred body, she'd watched the transformation during the succession of regen treatments during which the body had fed on its own available materials in an attempt to facilitate its healing. She had seen the inevitable retrograde development, until the flesh was flawlessly golden as it must have been before, until the breasts were wideset ice

97

cream cones barely large enough to fill a hand. She had monitored the specially prepared subliminal recordings that had changed the girl's personality pattern to match her new physical structure, while she slept.

She was the same person. The same collection of genes. But magically altered. A child, with the vague memories of an adult past.

Just a kid who needs help, Evelyn told herself. The girl would grow up again into a new life, unconnected with the creche. Another complication; the legal technicalities of her creche-less maturation would take time to work out. Lorna would have to be raised as a Sponje, a Sponsored Juvenile. As soon as they had the papers.

Evelyn shook her head. She'd leave that to the legal eagles. Her job was to go get the breakfast tray, for starters.

Although she'd been completely familiar with the city previously, Lorna now saw it through different eyes and with different emotional interpretations. As they toured the metropolis, Evelyn was learning the difficult art of keeping this newly evolved teen-ager in control. She kept a firm grip on Lorna's hand to restrain her from giddy digressions.

When they entered a restaurant for lunch, Evelyn sat back with a sigh. Under the table she pushed off her shoes with her feet. Lorna wanted everything; they settled that, eventually.

They were halfway through the meal when the strange voice abruptly interrupted Lorna's sparkling—and often overloud—observations.

"May I see your sponsor papers, please?"

Evelyn froze with her fork half raised. Her mind raced frantically. Who'd have thought, who'd have dreamed—but she had to have an answer, and fast. She lowered the fork in what she hoped was a leisurely manner, glancing up at the uniformed woman. Evelyn smiled.

"I'm sorry. I don't carry the papers. I'm a registered nurse, you see, and this girl is my charge."

98

The policewoman clucked her tongue sympathetically. "Do you have your nurse I.D., then?"

"Oh, yes." Evelyn snatched the card from her belt-pouch.

The policewoman examined it, nodded, and handed it back. "Thank you. But the sponsor should have supplied you with a dupe certificate. Certainly a nurse must be aware of the government's concern for the welfare of children. There are too few of them, these days. What would you have done if this girl had become lost and you'd had to have authoritative material to help us locate her?"

The food she'd eaten was not sufficient to keep Evelyn's stomach from feeling suddenly very empty. "Would a viz to the doctor be sufficient? I'm sure he can clear this up quickly." *Why do cops always enjoy making you sweat so? You're so concerned about brats, butch-bitch, have some!*

Butch-bitch was shaking her head, looking very sorrowful; they always did. "Not really, without the sponsor's papers. I'm really sorry, but—can you tell me where the sponsor can be reached?"

"Good grief, no." Evelyn tried to laugh. "He's on an extended business trip."

The woman stared at her a moment, then swung her eyes to Lorna. "What's your sponsor's name, child?

"I'm not a child."

"Would you answer me please?"

"Uh . . . Wesley—" she began/"George . . ." Evelyn began.

Silence. The policewoman stared at them, then nodded grimly and raised an eyebrow at Evelyn. "I'm afraid I'm going to have to take the girl into custody. Temporarily, of course." She handed Evelyn a card. "My name, number, and station. The legal sponsor can regain custody of the child by appearing with proper I.D. and proof of sponsorship. I'm really very sorry about this, but children are the most valuable citizens in the League, and you're both aware they are wards of the government until they reach adult status." She glanced at Lorna. "I'd judge that to be several years off."

"I know all that," Evelyn said, wondering what the femcop's reaction would be if she were told the "child" was in her late twenties. But—there was no way of proving even that. The situation was so complicated that only a battery of lawyers could straighten it out. That or a lot of money—maybe. Bitch-butch's assertions about Gov's concern for children was genuine enough. It had taken a while, but the solution to the old population explosion was inevitably leading to an implosion problem.

Noticing the expression of innocent bewilderment on Lorna's face, she knew she had to try.

"Look, dragging this girl out of here and putting her in a creche among strangers will have an effect on her mind I'd hate to consider. Are you ready to take that responsibility?"

"I am charged with the protection of the citizenry," she was told. "Push me a little more and I'll stop trying to protect you and call a car to run you downtown."

"How in blazes can dragging this girl away from me serve the state? And how can you justify it with Freewill?"

"The ways of Gov are not mine to question," the policewoman said. "It works in many ways its task to perform."

Evelyn bit her lip, then reached out to grasp Lorna's hand. "Honey, listen closely. She's going to creche you until this is straightened out. Keep your mind clear, and don't worry. That's very important; *act your age* at all times and please be a good girl."

"Come along, dear," the policewoman smiled. "Please don't be frightened. I'm not near as mean as I look."

Lorna bounced to her feet and threw her arms around Evelyn's neck, kissing her full on the lips. She smiled sunnily. "Don't worry, Evelyn. I'll be good—I'll act my age. Come for me as soon's you can."

The nurse watched them leave the restaurant, Lorna's hand firmly enclosed by the policewoman's. The moment they were gone, Evelyn leaped to her feet. Forgetting her shoes, she ran past staring eaters to a visiphone booth. She tapped out the code as fast as she could. And fidgeted, biting and licking her lips until the face of Doctor Eversole appeared.

"I lost her!"

He stared at her, immediately alert. "What happened?"

"The completely unexpected. This long witch of a femcop showed up and asked for the sponsor papers. There aren't any! She took her into custody. Doctor, what do I do-o-o-o—" and she was weeping.

He forced himself to relax so that all she saw was the confident smile of reassurance she needed. "You call me just as you have, and I call Blake and the Guild attorneys. Did the officer give you an I.D. card?"

"Yes. She was nice about it, I guess, but—"

"Um-hm. Come on back here to the hospital, Evelyn, and we'll get things moving toward her release. Damn! Don't expect it to be in a hurry, though. We haven't, as the saying goes, a leg to stand on. We'll probably have to wait while they check the records on all three League planets, then decide to wait for every ship in space to planetfall so they can check the passengers. And if we interfere, try to volunteer any information—we're in trouble, sure as I sit here. *Damn*! This could take months, Evelyn."

"Oh my god . . ."

"Where is a girl safer than in a creche? She'll learn the proper behavior there. You've said she was all right, well oriented. This isn't the end of the world."

"That poor girl . . ."

"Flash off, Evelyn. I'm calling Blake now."

Evelyn stood there in the vizbooth and wept. In her stocking feet.

TWELVE...

Harriet adjusted the skin-tight swimsuit, reaching inside to tuck herself carefully, more comfortably into the left cup. She smoothed the yellow plastifab over her hips, surveying herself in the mirror; the suit's contrast against her dark flesh was magnificent. She laughed, knowing she'd attract her share of male attention.

"Poor jackos! Oh well, at least I'm giving them a look. They can get their real flashes from the real heifers."

The big spaceliner was well on its way on the long journey to Mars. Harriet had plenty of time to relax now, to forget the odious visit to Earth, and she meant to make the most of this hiatus in a life that had become increasingly hectic since she'd first met Roland Balearic. Her eyes narrowed as she thought of that, and she paused, staring at the mirror, thinking of their meeting.

"They're beautiful," she had said, reaching out to touch the stones.

Balearic had withdrawn the gems quickly. "Better not touch them with your bare hands. They affect some women . . . . strangely. Which is the whole point, of course. But they won't kill anyone. Not in this dimension, anyhow."

"Dimension!" She had stared at the flat-eyed man. So he'd decided to play the mystery role! She had attacked it at once: "What kind of vut is that? Look, jacko. You offer a good deal, and my percentage sounds pos, but I'm

102

not going to peddle some fobby story along with it and risk psyconditioning!"

Smilingly condescendingly, he returned the gems to their box.

"Citizen," he'd said, because she was after all Martian, and they were more formal than Earth-types. "I assure you that you will not have to peddle the story. Only the jewels. As to the word 'dimension,' I use it only to simplify. Universe would be nearer the truth. One of an infinity of universes coexistent with this one, but separate. I intend to conquer a universe."

The statement was absurd; it was prodigiously absurd in a restaurant booth. Harriet laughed. "With a bunch of baubles? What are you going to do, stone them to death?"

"Precisely." Roland sipped at his wine and licked his lips in appreciation. "I cannot be insulted, citizen, so feel free to cast whatever aspersions make you feel superior. Consider me a lunatic if it pleases you. Even a sadistic scoundrel. As to these items: we will market them under the name 'Star Pearls.'"

"But they're jewels, not pearls."

"So they are. It has a nice sound that will appeal. There will be even greater appeal when they learn there's a bit of danger in owning one of these. Women, I mean, not lesbies."

"You're right about that," she said. "Lesbies aren't as stupid as ordinary women. They'd never fall for that nonsense." She eyed him curiously. "How is it a rock prospector knows so much? You never came on like this when you were casing Wildcat Row for a courier. Everybody had the impression you were a little simple-minded."

Balearic nodded. "Exactly the impression I wished to create. I was interested in a courier willing to take long chances. I believe I have taken every eventuality into consideration, but this sort of market can fluctuate without warning. Gems have more emotional value than practical, and emotions can be dangerous to financial ventures. I guarantee first payment, citizen, but after that everything depends on our ability to work together in the . . . coordination of this operation."

Harriet nodded, scratching her thigh. "I'll take a chance, so long as that first payment's guaranteed. But why take them so far away as Earth? Why not market them on Mars?"

The man with the unwavering gray eyes shook his head. "Too close to the source. The authorities may eventually be some trouble, and there are a few things I'd rather they never know. Ordinarily, we would avoid the jurisdiction of the Terran League. The area where I found these contains a mass of unbelievable ancient ruins, you see—which would classify it as an architectural find, and I would have no claim." He chuckled, softly. He always seemed in perfect control; each gesture, each wan smile, each soft laugh. And the eyes. "I am evading the controls of the law, for the moment. They are welcome to the location after I am finished with this operation."

Harriet shrugged. "Evasion of laws is part of the business. But—" She studied him. "I keep wondering if I should be afraid of you."

He nodded without changing his expression. "Definitely."

She laughed. "Well, let's talk about the split. Mind going over that once more? And recording? I really don't believe it."

"I realize my 'terms' are difficult to believe. All I want out of this is operating costs. All profit is yours."

She shook her head. "You really aren't kidding."

"No." Balearic remained calm as he watched her astonishment. "I am incapable of kidding. You do agree the stones are marketable?"

"With the right promotion," she told him—and herself, for confidence, "anything can be marketed. Jewels are a cinch." She eyed him suspiciously. "But what the vut are you getting out of this?"

"A universe, as I said," he said perfunctorily. "The stones are not what they appear to be, citizen. They are the parts of a life generator of an entire civilization. Of many civilizations, in fact. Through proper reassembly of these . . . components, I am reprogramming a device

104

that will generate . . . a complete dislocation of mental processes."

His half-smile, the implausibility of the story, and her own greed made her wonder. Was it all just sauce? What sort of weapons could baubles be?

"If you hadn't shown me materially marketable goods, little friend, I'd walk right out of here and forget the whole thing."

His nod appeared triumphant. "Of course you would. I am fully cognizant of the facts of human nature—which is my reason for proceeding this way." He took out a wallet and counted out that strange commodity one so seldom saw: cash. League notes. "That should constitute a sufficiently binding advance."

Harriet had the bills counted and out of sight in seconds. She gazed across the little table into his devitalized eyes. "I still think you're fobby, but it's a deal. You supply the cargo and I'll handle it from there, partner."

And they had begun. And wound up on Earth, with the horror of that completely inoffensive girl with the superb body, and now they were fugitives, en route to Mars, and Harriet was accessory to . . . whatever. Had the girl died? Was the charge murder, or interference with Freewill plus assault? Whatever, capture meant psycho-conditioning, if not worse. And she was certainly going to do some fancy relaxing on this trip!

Flying her own ship in total secrecy for over a year and a half had kept her far out of touch with normal activities—normal, that is, for her. Now that the big ship was settling down to standard cruise routine, she was sure that the best place to evaluate female partner potential was in the pool. She left her oversize suite.

The appreciative glances and low whistles from the males she passed brought a smile to her lips. She ambled into the great chamber housing the pool, and had to grin, wondering: what would be the reaction of all these silly water cavorters if the gyros went on the bash and the water balled and floated?

Some were swimming, but most of the bodies were seeking, as she was, flesh fields of conquest. She watched a beautifully curved brunette dive gracefully from the board, her body arching across the enormous mural depicting the Western galaxy. Wondering if that girl with her long, long hair was available, Harriet felt the touch on her calf. She looked down to see a dark-haired Cauc—male—resting on one arm on the pool's edge. His other hand traced the curve of her leg.

He grinned. "Hi, brown sugar. What's your pleasure for the trip?"

She laughed. "You're wasting your time, friend. I don't dig men."

"Neither do I," he assured her, without rancor. "I sure dig legs, though, and you've got your share. Sure you won't change your spots?"

She shook her head. "Not a chance, jacko. You and I are competitors."

"Ah, what a sad and enormous pity." He sighed dolorously, eyeing her. "Well, at least you gave me the pleasure of looking at you. See any good prospects among these water babies, competitor?"

Since he wasn't going to push, Harriet relaxed and sat down, thrusting her feet into the water. "I just got here. But the brunette who just dived in looks . . . intriguing."

"Forget it. Captain's mistress."

"How do you know?"

"I work here," he grinned. "Bartender. Right now I'm off duty for the next eight hours, and I'm doing just what you are: looking for a good flash. Name's Roscoe. Been to the Sappho Lounge yet?"

"Negative, and I'm Harriet. I stay away from unfamiliar lezbars. Too many dykes think I'm a fairyfemme because of my looks, and that always leads to trouble. I'm big enough to slap 'em down if they push it, but I don't like to waste the effort. And don't look at me that way, jacko. If you were standing beside me, you'd know better. I'm five ten, in my bare feet."

"How tall are you in your bare body?"

She laughed. "You're not about to find out, jacko!"

He sighed, then suddenly pointed across the pool. "There's your gal."

106

Harriet's eyes followed his pointing finger with interest. "Cutesy blonde near the corner of the pool? What makes you so sure, paisano?"

"Experience. I've been on this run eight years. I know the possibilities. Besides—blondes like you dark types. Contrast. You look like you had parents of pure stock on both sides. Black mama maybe, white daddy? That where you got the Cauc features and the pretty brown bod?"

"Give it up, Roscoe. We were talking about that blonde."

"Um. She's in no hurry. Been standing there in the shallow section quite a while, looking the place over. I'll give you odds she's AC-DC."

"So why don't you take her?"

"I just might—" Roscoe looked up at her abruptly, wearing a broad grin. "Why don't we both?"

"Oh, stand by, jacko, d'you thing I'd share with a *man*?"

"Why not?" He shrugged, his face a study in innocence. "I'm real generous."

"And loaded to the eyeballs with gall. You just want to see me bare."

"Welll . . . that's part of the plot. Can't see why I shouldn't kill two birds with one stone. Why should we—experts—make two girls a little happy when we can give one heifer the thrill of her life?"

Harriet leaned back, rocking with laughter. "Brother, do you have an imagination!" She eyed the blonde with a raised eyebrow. "It does have possibilities, doesn't it. After all, I'm not looking for a permanent thing—and I'm not a manhater." She turned deep chocolate eyes on him. "You're on, Roscoe. Let's see what we can make of this."

She bounced up and dived cleanly into the water. As she swam smoothly across the pool, Roscoe kept pace with seeming effortlessness, his lean arms cutting the water with smooth, casual strokes. When she disappeared, he, too, submerged in her wake.

Harriet surfaced, shook her head once, and braced

107

herself against the pool's edge. Breathing heavily, she wiped the water from her eyes with one hand. Then she grinned at the blonde, less than two feet away and watching the heaving of her bosom above the yellow swimsuit. Harriet blinked; she hadn't realized from across the pool that what the blonde girl wore was paint, cleverly applied.

"Hi, sugar. Looking for me?"

The girl's hand went to her throat. Her eyes widened in surprise. Then she caught herself and gazed primly across the pool, brows arched. "Not that I've noticed."

Roscoe rose on the other side of her. "How about me, kitten?" He leaned around her. "Hi, Harry!"

"Hey, Roscoe. She found us."

The girl looked frantically from one to the other of her flankers, then began a laugh that devolved into a giggle. "Where did you two come from?"

"Other side of the pool," Harriet said, pulling herself up onto the poolside. "We thought you looked lost, so we came over to tell you where you are."

"That's right," Roscoe nodded. "We came hurrying over to tell you you're on a pleasure trip. Now don't you feel better?"

"No! I feel . . ." The girl's fingers rose to toy with her suit, and one bare-nippled touch reminded her she wore none. She jerked her hand from the purple-painted breast. "Who *are* you two bugs?"

"Now we're making some progress, beautiful! That's Harry, and she's a lesbie, and I'm Roscoe, and I'm not. What do you do for fun?"

She gave first him, then Harriet, a sidelong look. Considered. Decided. "I'm Ginger. And for fun I try to figure out how I get caught in the middle of nefarious plans."

Harriet touched the girl's chin, gently turning her head. She didn't miss the flicker of Ginger's eyes, or the flare of her nostrils.

"Why, sugar . . . nefarious? Whatever gave you that idea?"

Within five minutes the arrangement had been made— Harriet's suite—and she and Roscoe were watching the girl as she ran undulantly to the dressing room. Roscoe grinned at Harriet.

"See, Harry? I was right. I'll collect some drinkables, on me, and meet you at your cabin."

Harriet nodded. Her big form straightened as she pushed her feet against the wall and—

closed and locked the safe, then turned to stare in horror into the muzzle of the needler

screamed in the fear of death as the little spacer spun uncontrollably toward the lunar surface

dived into the pool, aware of the female eyes on his well-developed and superbly-tanned body

—stroked smoothly across the pool, contemplating the pleasures soon to come. Roscoe and Ginger; what a pair, what a pair of *names!*

From the lounge chair in the balcony overlooking the pool, Roland Balearic watched the brown woman in the yellow suit with narrow-eyed intensity. He had covered his astonishment; she was surfacing! That settled it.

He'd have to kill her.

THIRTEEN...

Policewoman Madhura had radioed in, so that the patrol car appeared as she and Lorna reached the corner down the street from the restaurant. Madhura opened the door and entered after Lorna, giving the driver the directions as she settled herself.

"Where . . . are you . . . taking me?"

"The nearest creche," Madhura said, pulling up the little ornament on a coilwire from her lapel. "The African one's closest; we certainly won't have any trouble locating you there!" She started dictating her report into the ornament.

Lorna bit her lip, watching the traffic with apprehensive eyes, carefully not-listening to Madhura's report. She folded her hands loosely in her lap, pouting. *Adults*, she thought, and her thought processes dissolved into a state of confusion as she tried to coordinate recollections of being aged twenty-seven with her present condition.

"You about fifteen, honey?" the policewoman asked.

"Um-hm." Lorna nodded. "Sixteen." And she believed it. Her psyconditioned mind was delighted to accept anything as positive; it was staggering under the load of too many maybes and once-weres and what-ifs.

"Do you know of any identifying marks you might have, Lorna?"

She shook her head. "There isn't one teensy mark on

me," she said. She was certain of that, too. She frowned; why was she certain?

The car flashed above the residential district and out into open country. Swinging off the traffic beam, the driver eased out above grass and trees until he cruised in toward a sudden complex of buildings and high walls that stretched across several acres of rolling countryside. He started down just as the two swift interceptors came for him. They escorted him to the ground. The next several minutes of careful scrutiny and counter-checking convinced Lorna that the estate would be very hard to sneak into. She wondered if it would be as difficult to leave.

Vague memories of such a place crept from the depths of her subconscious. This was a creche, one of many dotting the three planets. Here were those all-too-few children birthed to mateslaves, raised and educated under the best conditions the Terran League offered.

She saw astonished face after astonished face as they approached the main building, then entered and walked along the hall into a foyer that was quite plain. The black woman behind the barrier of the counter was no exception. She looked no less astonished as Madhura told her about Lorna.

"Don't you think you're in the wrong place?"

Madhura shook her head. "Merely temporary; you were nearest. And I honestly think there may be something strange here. Your creche would be a hard place for Lorna to get lost in."

The woman laughed. "I'll agree to that! Well, there'll have to be a routine check, all the way around. We'll start here, officer."

Madhura nodded. "Good. We'll be in contact." She patted Lorna on the cheek. "Now don't you worry, ch— Lorna. Everything will be all right."

Lorna watched her go, feeling abandoned. And overdressed. Everyone she'd seen here wore nothing but a lot of brown or black skin. Including the woman behind the counter. She bit her lip.

"Don't look so lost, Lorna," she said. "We'll try to

111

make your stay here as happy as possible. The League always looks after its children." She flashed the brilliant smile Lorna thought was so friendly. "Of course, it's a little unusual, your being *here*. But I think it's a wonderful idea. All the national creches are integrated, and why the international ones aren't I can't imagine. Of course, if the sponsor matter turns out to be correct, you won't be here long enough to learn anything, so we won't assign you to classes. My name is Annette, by the way. Just Annette."

"You may as well assign me to classes," Lorna said. "I don't have any sponsor. I'm—"

"What? You—" Annette gazed at her, astounded. "Then where—where do you belong, Lorna?"

Lorna shook her head. She felt the tears coming, tried to stop them, couldn't. She couldn't remember. Her head hurt, and she couldn't remember where she belonged. And she was getting scared.

She said so, all of it.

Annette came quickly out to hug her. She patted Lorna's back, crooning. The girl clung to her and sobbed. "You poor, poor baby. We'll take care of you, little Lorna-Lorna. You'll be fine. Would you like something to eat?"

Lorna nodded against the woman, feeling overdressed again, and then she fought to stem her tearflow as she pushed herself back. "Ann—Annette? Should I . . . shouldn't I be . . . I feel funny, dressed!"

Annette laughed. "Good! You'll be fine, sweetheart; you adapt easily, don't you? Yes, you just get like everyone else around here, and I'll find you a pair of sandals. That's all anyone wears here, and most of the kids don't bother with them. Footwear's about as important as underwear, did you know that?"

No, Lorna didn't know that, but she seemed to remember having spent a great deal of time without either clothing or footwear. She stripped easily, unconcernedly; it was easier in a place where she knew no one else wore clothing. But she accepted the sandals Annette gave her. Annette remarked on the firmness and above all the whiteness of her breasts (they were not white, of course, just as Lorna wasn't; no one was).

Lorna chuckled, walking beside the slender black woman. "I hope it doesn't bother everybody here," she said. "Gosh, I never knew real black people had black nipples, too."

Annette laughed. Lorna giggled. Her conscious mind swam for its life on the dark sea of her subconscious, and memory after memory sank down through the murk. The happy thoughts rose; the others vanished. The creche was happiness and forgetfulness, a retreat.

They were in the open and walking, down a tree-lined path. Scattered at what appeared to be random intervals amid the trees and shrubbery were two-story houses of various designs. There would be no regimentation that might adversely affect the development of crechelings into individual adults.

"This way, Lorna," Annette said, turning down a path leading to a house designed in imitation of the 19th- or 20th-century style called "Victorian." As she mounted the steps, Lorna saw that even the window curtains were in the same style. She gasped as they entered an apt—no, *house*—that breathed femininity. From the light perfume fragrances, the colors, the frills, there was no doubt that the place had been planned for female residency and that only.

She clapped her hands at her own apartment.

Annette waved a hand about the main room. "It's all yours as long as you're with us, Lorna. I wish we had more kids—we have plenty of empty suites. It's your job to keep this place as clean and neat as it is right now; the instruction book for the cleaning robots is right here. Come along downstairs, dear, and we'll catch the dieticians offguard. They'll have something to talk about for days!"

With an indecorous squeal of delight, the naked white girl followed the naked black woman.

After lunch, she hurried back upstairs to her own apt. She gave the door a push behind her, kicking off her sandals to run and stretch on the canopied bed. She bounced there, enjoying the feel of it and the loveliness

113

of the room, loving the thought that it was *hers*. She had no idea what to do with herself, and it did not bother her in the least.

The lessons would require four hours daily, seven days a week. Extra time was required for failure to meet minim-Ed requirements. Group activities seemed to be going on constantly, but they were not mandatory. Nothing was. Don't like English? How about history? Don't like that? What about mechanics, then? No? Tried horticulture or cooking?

Drowsily, she toyed with her fading memories. She wondered if she could still cuss, and she tried; the words sounded silly before they passed her lips. Giggling, she buried her face in the lace-trimmed pillow and drifted into sleep . . .

. . . and woke with a start when the door banged open. A small brown body raced across the room.

"Welcome to Nigeria, Lorna!"

"Nigeria?"

"Sure—all the houses have names, silly. Hey, you *are* a pale one!" The girl kicked off her sandals, then jumped up and knelt bouncily on the bed beside Lorna.

"Hi. I'm Patricia. I'm ten, and I've finished all my lessons for today and Annette told me about you and I came to see for myself if you're really that pretty." She placed a brown hand on Lorna's stomach. "Hey, *that* looks pretty!" Suddenly, her hand moved downward. "Oh! Your lips're pink—how's your clitty?" And she found it expertly.

Lorna groaned and snapped her thighs together—and let them sigh apart again. She tried weakly to close them, but found that her body knew what it wanted far better than her mind. Her breathing quickened. The room's temperature seemed to shoot up.

"Wh-what . . . d'you think y-you're d-*doing*, you twerp?"

Patricia giggled. "Somebody has to start you off right. This is where we learn to be adults, and this is what they do, dummy. You're here to *learn*, remember? I happen to be the expert around here, mainly because I'm too young for anything else. Relax and enjoy it."

Relaxing wasn't easy, but Lorna enjoyed it.

114

Very late in the afternoon, Patricia led Lorna downstairs and onto the front porch. Eyes stared. Her pale Cauc-ness stood out with such startling clarity among the other girls that she was more than a little ill at ease. She felt like the only banjo in a ukulele band. Nor did it help matters when Patricia shouted:

"Hey, kids, this is *Lorna*! Boy, does she *ecstat*! Boy, can she DO IT!"

Lorna's face flamed. Her reaction was instantaneous: she delivered a stinging slap across Patricia's backside. "Do you have to tell everything?"

Words-action-words brought a round of applause. The busty girl on the railing, black and shiny as though she'd been polished, waved.

"Now you're in the group, Lorna. Patricia's our pet. She's the best—and she also has the biggest mouth in creche. She also teases boys." She glanced sternly at Patricia. "Trouble is, it's the big boys she teases, and one of these days she's going to be sorrr-reee."

Patricia was sitting on the steps, strapping her sandals. She giggled. "Oh, no, Monica. I run too fast."

Monica shrugged. "Some day you're going to trip, baby-doll, and get yourself fence-posted." She smiled at Lorna. "Want to meet some boys tonight?"

Patricia swung around, her face very serious. "Don't rush her, Monnie. She's been in a hospital, and she's tight as a drum."

Lorna rolled her eyes. "Oh Pat*ricia*!"

Monica slid off the railing and hurried over to kiss Lorna on the cheek. "Sorry, honey. I didn't know you'd been revirginated." She dropped a hand on Lorna's shoulder and grinned. "But you're going to have to lose it some-time. Can't give up fun forever. That's what creches are all about. It ain't the *formal* lessons that make adults out of us!"

"Uh . . . maybe . . . if somebody's nice and gentle . . ."

Monica laughed and hugged her. "I can pick *just* the right boy for that."

"She's had *lots* of experience," another girl said.

115

"Big deal," Patricia snapped. "At fifteen she's a regular woman of the world." She ducked Monica's swat with nimble ease, grinning.

Monica snatched up the pillow from one of the old-fashioned chairs. "Go on and tease the boys, shrimp. You're downing a serious conversation between us big kids."

Laughing, Patricia sidestepped the hurtling pillow, then bounced down the steps and ran along the path. The girls gasped, then looked at each other as a tall boy appeared and sprinted after her.

"That's David! She's been giving him a hard time for a week."

"I hope she trips! Time she became a woman. I was nine."

"How old are you, Lorna? Wow, really? You Caucs develop slow, huh? But what happened that put you in hospital?"

"Sunady!"

Sunady looked guiltily at Monica, then smiled at Lorna. "Sorry. Forget I asked." She glanced over her shoulder. "Hey, was that yell our Patricia?"

They didn't see Patricia until dinner: she came in, walking slowly and carefully, her eyes faraway. She grunted as she sat down.

"Hey—Patricia! What's fobbing you?"

"I tripped," the girl said, in a dazed voice.

Soft shadows of a moonlit evening blanketed the creche and faint sounds of music, vagrant snatches of conversation and ripples of laughter drifted among the widely separated houses. The pattering quickstep of sandals and bare feet echoed in the twilight as Monica and Lorna walked along a shrub-flanked path. As they passed through a patch of shade, Monica's jet body nearly vanished, giving the impression that Lorna walked alone.

Monica laughed. "You'd sure have a hard time hiding around here, you know?"

Lorna nodded. "I feel like I'm in a spotlight. I hope it doesn't make the boys nervous."

116

Monica grinned, raising an eyebrow as lasciviously as she was capable. "Huh! I hope it doesn't make *you* nervous, seeing a bunch of self-contained pole vaulters." She touched Lorna's arm. "But don't worry. I promised I'd introduce you to a gentle boy, and I will. If anybody else gets you got before then, well . . . do something else." Laughing easily, she pointed to a small building down a side path. "That's one of the lower-level entrances, in case you have to make a dash out of the rain."

Lorna shrugged. "What difference does it make, rain on skin?"

"I don't know, that's the way people are. It rains and everybody heads for cover. Anyhow, there're sublevel entrances in each house. They're really handy in winter. There are seven belowground levels, and the only way down is the elevators. We don't waste time on the first level down; that's just kitchens and supplies. Classrooms are on two, libraries on three. Fourth and fifth levels are recreation. Six—now there's the place. It's orientation-transition, for everyone going through Rites and leaving the creche. Seven's just the machinery that keeps the place going." The tall girl gripped her wrist. "That's the layout, Lorna, now we'll see about the lay."

They approached a brownstone, partially concealed by broad-branched trees. Through the leaves several windows glowed with soft inner light, sprinkling the surrounding shrubbery with pale white and yellow. The two Af boys on the porch waved; Monica waved back. She trotted up the steps and enveloped one of them with her arms, giving him a long kiss. The other boy was gazing at Lorna with his brows up.

"Who's the shy ghost, Monnie?"

Monica freed her lips and gasped for air. "Lorna. She's sixteen and you be careful. She just came out of hospital with a new guesswhat."

"Flasherino!" He raised his hands in horror, rolling his eyes at the starry sky. "A virgie in the creche? This is *sacrilege*!"

Not quite certain why, Lorna felt quite ashamed.

117

It was purely accidental, surely. Policewoman Madhura probably had something on her mind. Lorna, maybe. But in the accident she was crushed into a hideous jellylike mess, and her recorder/reporter was a part of that mess.

FOURTEEN...

Where did I get a mind like this? Who—what am I?

Wesley Harmon had started out with the intention of killing two people. But his own mind was steadily contributing complications that seemed somehow related to what they'd done to Lorna.

His *own* mind?

He was sure it was, just as he knew he should be able to identify the robed woman in the flaming vision; just as he knew he would understand what had happened after the demolition of the two planets. He had the frustrated feeling that pieces of the puzzle were being held just out of his reach, suspended in the recesses of his subconscious —yet used like a carrot before a horse, drawing him on and on. *As if my subconscious mind weren't really mine.*

But the ship was; he had the record of Manny's last words. He checked out the cargo, opened one of the "hot" crates, and lifted out one of the neutron rifles and a box of charges. Then he resealed the crate and rearranged it among the others. Where he was going, he'd need a gun that would fire in airless space, where the .45 would be useless. Why and how he knew, did not occur to him. (Had the thought been born, it would have been obliterated before it developed. His mind smoothly circumvented the forbidden area and attached itself to the present positive.)

Obviously the shipment was illegal, which was why it

119

had been sent out on a wildcatter. Private citizens were not permitted zappers. Covering his own theft would be diabolically simple, and good citizenship to boot.

(*enjoyed the warmth of Tommy's body against his as she slept in his arms*)

The remainder of his journey to Mars was uneventful, and he was delighted when the time at last came when he was needed. That, too, was simple; he contacted the freeport outside Urbanova, arranged for docking facilities, reported Manuel's death, and began his descent. He had made arrangements with a local hauler to pick up his shipment even before he was berthed.

He made another call, and watched with mild amusement as the cargo was towed away. That would be one surprised pair of haulers when the local authorities stopped them and confiscated their load. In their elation, surely the Martian cops would not notice one missing rifle.

He returned to the cargo hold with his payment, wondering what to do with it. He knew Manuel had distrusted banks, and kept his money ever with him, in a box in the hold. Wes stared when he had sprung it open. It was packed almost to the top with League currency. He separated out a few bills, tossed the rest back, and closed the lid. Then he strolled leisurely through the ship—

(humming a tune that had died millenia before . . . millenia before . . .)

—and stepped through the airlock. He secured it and walked without hurrying toward Wildcat Row.

He ordered steak and eggs in a half-empty café, delighted to pay the fantastic price after the monotony of the artificials he'd been living on ever since he'd left Earth. He was working on the steak when a man in a crumpled jacsuit walked in and sat down two tables away, near the counter.

"Hey, Barney," he called to the counterman. "Manny Schultheis been in lately?"

Barney shook his head. "Hallo, Phineas. No, he hasn't. His ship in?"

Wes said quietly, "Forget him. He's dead."

He raised his hands when they both swung to stare.

120

"We came up together from Earth. We ran into a load of god's garbage halfway here, and Manny went outside to check the hull. I've got it on tape."

"Jeeze, what a way to go!"

Wes nodded. "I had to listen to it. He didn't die right away. It's not pleasant to listen to a guy opening his own faceplate."

They were silent for a moment before Phineas nodded and came over. "Well, in that case you own the ship, now. I'm a cargo broker; my card. I've got a load of film that I want to get to——"

"Phineas, you are a callous turd. Get scarce."

Phineas's bit would have been to stare, to bluster, to point out who and what he was to this wildcatter. He didn't. He departed without a word, leading Wes to assume things were still just as wild as always on Mars's Wildcat Row. Phineas had not blustered for the simple reason that he might well have been beaten up or shot where he stood.

But he popped his head back in the door, calling to Barney. "Hey, Barn . . . when's the last time you saw Harry?"

Barney shook his head. "Been over a year, Phineas, ever since she grabbed that Hidalgo thing everybody else was turning down."

Wes looked up, waiting with his back to Phineas until Barney's actions indicated that the cargo broker had this time exited for good. Then Wes asked, "Hidalgo? Why'd anyone want to go out *there*, Barney? That's the most cockeyed asteroid in the system."

Barney grinned. "Harriet's a little cockeyed herself. Who are you—and have you really got a tape of Manny getting it?"

Wes rose and carried his plate and cup to the counter. "More coffee, please," he said, straddling a stool. "I'm Wes Harmon, Barney, and I'm showing I.D. because I understand your . . . interest. Yes, I really have a tape. It's on deposit with Berthmaster; call the field."

Barney tested him by going over to the viz and flicking it on, then turning suddenly to look at Wes. Wes sat where he was, waiting. The counterman nodded, switched off the viz, and returned. He drew the coffee.

"Manny was strictly all right, Harmon. How well'd you know him?"

Wes scratched his nose. "Met him at the field outside Megaterra when I bought on from a man named Izzy Vanipoor in Eddie's. For five thou. After that I knew him as well as you can, crammed into Miss Scotty for about a half-flight."

Barney sighed. "All right. You asked a question. Some nutty prospector was after someone to haul and peddle stuff he dug up, out in the asteroids. Turned out to be Hidalgo. You say it's cockeyed—right, and Harriet isn't." He grinned. "She's a super-wildcat, a spacer good as any man and big enough so no one denies it. Also a lesbie. She—"

"She a black heifer?"

"Right. You know her, then."

Wes shook his head. "About twenty-eight, isn't she? Unless she's a regen."

"She isn't," Barney said, rolling his eyes. "And what a waste all that bod is! No, that's about her age, a baby." He grinned. "Me, I'm ninety-one. Been through twice. Anyhow, Harry'll try anything once. So she gave this prospector nut the nod, and when somebody said something smart, I had to replace two tables and the chair she creamed him with. She doesn't give anyone a chance."

"Yeah," Wes said quietly. "What about the prospector?"

"Looked like anything else but! No one would go along with him because this is a quick-cash business and he wouldn't say what he had; just that he'd make someone a millionaire. You know how *that* struck everybody— they laughed and ordered another drink. *All* prospectors are going to get rich and make somebody else the same. But nobody has to buy into a blind deal. There's always plenty of quick wildcat business, cash."

"He had to've had his own ship," Wes prompted. He didn't dare touch his coffee cup, or even show his hands. He was having trouble controlling himself. He'd found his people—or at least, he knew who one of them was.

Harriet. Big and black and young and Martian and lesbie. And she and her contractee were the Star Pearl suppliers. Now all he had to do was try to get as much scrute as he could without blowing his fobs.

Barney was chuckling. "Yeah, he had a ship, if you want to call it that! A real antique, with in-line field coils, looked like it was going to blow up in port. Damned if I know how he ever got clear out to Hidalgo—and back. And like I said, he looked about as much like a prospector as Phineas, the turd." He grinned. "I liked that. So would Manny, Wes. Where is he?"

"Where he lived," Wes said.

"Yeah. He'd have liked that. Just spinning around out there, forever. Yeah. Uh . . . oh. You interested in this scuttlebutt?"

"A big sexy she-pilot with a million-dollar deal? Sure I'm interested. Don't all of us think we're going to be millionaires—and don't we all think we're going to show the lesbies the error of their ways?"

Barney grinned. "Yeah. Well, the prospector's name was Balearic—here, wait a min." He opened a drawer under the counter, rummaged, and came up with a very crumpled piece of paper, a strip off something else. He shook his head over it.

"*Roland* Balearic, isn't that nice? Here's where he started to write something else, then scratched it out. Never have figured it out. Looks like Chinese, but none of my ancestors could read it, and I'll bet on it. Here. Ever see anything like this?"

Wes took the crumpled and aged strip of paper and examined it casually (but his inner reaction was less than nonchalant. The not-quite obliterated writing was in an alphabet and a language that had died millenia in the past with the flaming demolition of a planet. The glyphs were barely pronounceable in any League dialect, but "Wesley" read it with ease, feeling a chill as he recognized . . . a *woman*'s name).

Smiling easily, he returned the piece of paper. "Looks like something he might have found out there on nine-forty-four. Or just scribbling to get his pen started."

"It was an antique, same as his ship," Barney said.

Wes didn't dare ask what the man looked like, even though it might well have been safe. Barney was accepting him, but he did not *know* him, and a stranger in a dead man's ship shouldn't ask too many questions anywhere—particularly in Wildcat Row.

"Speaking of starting," he said, "I've got to get started on some serious drinking." He chucked one of the new League bills at Barney; Wildcat Row on Mars was not a cred-type town. "Keep it, Barney. Have a drink or two for Manny when you get off—and on him."

He sauntered out of the place and onto the dusty still walk—

and stored away the money and tossed the paper back into the drawer and closed it

and savored the delicious male taste as her contract sent his tongue exploring and

(*fingers touching the firing studs as the ship began to approach the surface of Hidalgo*)

—and walked to the nearest Wildcat Row bar, reflecting on the now-irrefutable evidence that what was happening was not a figment of his imagination. Without thinking about it, he softly whistled a tune that had died millenia before Ur of the Chaldees had crawled up from the mud of the Euphrates.

Harriet was stowing away her swimsuit when she heard the buzz. She headed toward the main room and the door, slipping her arms into a dressing gown and tying the sash with deft fingers. The pale blue robe billowed around her, lacy folds rippling and flowing with her long-legged litheness. She opened the door to grin at Ginger. She had removed her paint and donned a loose, sleeveless tunic that was open up both sides and fastened with ornamental clasps at each hip.

The diminutive blondé set one foot tentatively forward, peeking into the suite. "Gawd, looks like captain's quarters. Is Roscoe here yet?"

"Not yet, sugar. Come on in." Harriet stepped back and

124

let one hand reach lazily out as Ginger entered. The girl shivered, then smiled.

"That feels nice, Harry."

Harriet laughed. "You mean this?"

"Oh, *yes*. That's lovely. Let's . . . are we waiting for Roscoe?"

Harriet smiled. "Who?"

But a few minutes later the dim bedroom of her suite was flooded with sudden light. Startled, both women twisted their necks to look doorward. Roscoe stared, leaning against the jamb with his arms full of bottles. His brows were up.

"Boy, are you two a pair of hot stashes! I thought this was going to be a team thing."

"Uh . . . we got . . . carried away."

Depositing the bottles on a perm-mounted dresser, he let his eyes follow—with mock horror—the trail of hastily abandoned clothing. "Yeah," he said, joining them.

"Here! Stick to Ginger, jacko!"

Roscoe chuckled. "It's always such a pleasure, trying to convert the heathen to the path of righteousness."

"Leave *my* paths alone," Harriet warned him. "You just—"

released the safety catch and nodded at his partner

"Get *out of the way*!" Harriet arched her hips, throwing Roscoe to one side, onto Ginger. He grunted, flailing: "*Sorry!*"

Ginger stared in astonishment as Harriet rolled off the bed to land on her feet and run. Her hands clawed open a dresser drawer, and she was running again, stark naked and bouncing, a brown streak across the room to the bedroom door. Without pausing, she hurled it open and dropped to one knee. Fire exploded from the muzzle of her pistol. A stream of impure energy lashed across the outer room.

Ginger was shrieking. Roscoe dragged her from the bed onto the floor, his eyes very wide. Needles hummed into the room, holing the pillows and sheet. Roscoe held the shuddering girl down.

The first of the two rippers was already on his knees,

clawing at where his stomach blazed from Harriet's first bolt. She was already moving, with a pantherine speed and litheness, her pistol pouring out more fire. The second man jerked his arms up, but the clawing fingers were still inches from his bubbling face when he dropped, squealing. Harriet was rolling, still triggering, making sure of the second man. He too sprawled, liquid flame eating at his body

(*trying to figure how she could have missed Harmon with a full clip of needles when he'd been a clear target*)

Harriet's naked breasts bounced as though suspended on invisible strings as she panted, gazing at the two dead assassins-to-be. She half turned to peer back. "Anybody hurt in here?"

Roscoe's head appeared above the edge of the bed. He stared wide-eyed at the bare brown amazon with the wisp-wreathed pistol.

"Just scared, Harry, scared as hell. What the vutting sauce *happened?*"

She waved a hand over the walleye, illuminating the bedroom. "Not sure myself. Two men came in with guns out. I seem to've killed them both. Put a few shots of hooch into Ginger so she won't hysteric, will you?"

"Yeah, and the same medicine for *my* hysterics, lady."

Harriet prowled, investigating swiftly. Neither man had I.D.—or anything else other than the spare needlepack. Label-less clothing. The door had been lasered open, and she shook her head. If he'd tried using that thing as a weapon . . .

"GunTek," she muttered. "Expert door-openers, expert enough to know better than to try using a laser as a weapon on a spaceship . . . and without I.D. or labels. GunTek. Who?" She chewed her lip, narrowing her eyes. "Well, when in doubt, charge!"

She went to the viz, punched, and told the robovoice the cabin she wanted. Roland Balearic looked startled as she grinned at him.

"Who's trying to kill me, partner?"

He stared. "Wh-why, Harriet . . . what happened?"

"No sauce, Roland. Answer!"

126

His face assumed a pained expression. "Harriet, you are over-excited. We are business partners. What reason would I have to kill you?"

"That's what I want to know. You have a permanent contract with GunTek, I know that. You cost them several men, trying to take out Harmon."

"Harriet! Hush that." He looked baffled, and once more she wished those eyes were easier to read. "What's GunTek have to do—"

"Look, partner," she said, gazing levelly at him, "these two look like GunTek liquidators to me, and you've dealt with GunTek. What do you know about the late unlamented bodies adorning my suite?"

"Two you say?"

"Yeah, two."

Roland's face was worried. "And they're both dead?"

"Dammit, ask them!" What gave him the right—and ability—to be so vutting bland and unconcerned all the time?

"Harriet, you're fobbed and jumping to delusions. This has been an unusual trip; your nerves are understandably frayed. I cannot blame you too much for hurling wild accusations, but do be careful." He appeared deep in thought. "You know . . . I really might be to blame."

"Well, that's a cool way of admitting attempted murder!" She showed him her gun. "How'd you like—"

He waved his hand. "I did not mean that, Harriet." Looking embarrassed, he glanced away. His teeth were in his lower lip. He turned back to her with a sigh of resignation. "I think I have been guilty of stupidity, Harriet. I entered a conversation with two men in the main lounge, and I'm afraid I may have let them know you were traveling with a large amount of money. It came up when I tried my hand at selling one of the gems, you see."

Harriet eyed him irresolutely. "Fine, fine. Just what a girl needs to make her nice and safe. Look, partner darling, just leave the selling to me as arranged, all right?"

"I'm terribly sorry, Harriet."

127

"You are indeed, Roland. You're the sorriest—"

Again he waved a hand, without appearing angry. "Harriet, we can't let those bodies be found. We can't afford the attention they'd attract."

Harriet sighed, trying to heave out her tension. "Yes, yes. I can handle it. Now keep your vutting mouth shut, Roland. I want to enjoy this flight, and trading shots with rippers isn't my idea of fun."

She buttoned him off, him and his maddening serenity. Returning to the bedroom, she accepted the drink Roscoe handed her. He handed Ginger her second.

"Guzzle this and relax, kitten. It's all over now." With a look at Harriet, he stepped around her to stand in the doorway. "Did you do all this lady? Remind me to treat you the sweetest, will you?"

Harriet shrugged. "They broke in, and both had guns. When a jacko has a gun, I assume he means to use it."

He nodded, shivering a little and coming back for a bite of the half-empty bottle. He was frowning when he looked at her. "Harriet? I didn't hear anything. How'd you know they were out there?"

"I—don't know," she admitted, returning his frown. "I just did." She shrugged. "A hunch, maybe. You've had hunches, haven't you?"

He nodded. "I've got one right now: that you're in for some trouble. You planning on mounting these two birds for exhibition, maybe?"

She gave him a little smile, one eyebrow up. "I'm betting two thou you can make them disappear. You take bets, Roscoe?"

He headed for the viz, closed the bedroom door on both women, and knocked thirty minutes later. The outer room was empty. There was no blood on the carpet, although he'd been unable to do anything about the scorched places. He even had pillows and sheets. Beaming, he nodded without a sound and pocketed the IP coupons she handed him, equally silent. Then he looked at his watch.

"That sure shot the vutting hell out of this party! I'm due at the bar in an hour and a half. How about us getting together again in about twenty hours?"

128

"I'm—"

"Hush, Ginger," Harriet said, walking to Roscoe with smooth strides. She hadn't bothered re-dressing, and he showed surprise at her kiss and consternation at the nudge of her breasts. "I'm really sorry about all this mess, Roscoe doll. But there's plenty of time left on this cruise. Let's all make the most of it."

He shrugged. "I'm two thou to the better, less two hun apiece for a couple of efficient friends. Things have happened before. The captain'll be delighted to know his crew tried so hard to keep him from having to worry about anything aside from his joygirl's . . . wanderlust. Don't worry about it, Harry—and above all, don't *you* worry, Ginger." He patted both women with easy intimacy and headed for the door. "Don't wear Ginger *completely* out," he said and departed.

As the door closed, Harriet sipped more bottled warmth and smiled at Ginger. "Now, sweetheart, let's relax. I'll bet you didn't dream you'd be trapped with a cannibal."

"She can't be killed," Roland Balearic told thin air. And listened, and:

"I don't *know* if it's the same as with Harmon . . . No, I keep telling you this universe is different, they repro— No, no. They don't *do* it that way! They have two s— Well, you'll believe it when you come through . . . Positive. I'll try to kill her again, but I will no longer guarantee the possibility. On Mars, yes."

Roland's face resumed its normal lines, and he gave his head a quick jerk, blinking. He swung to the viz.

"Special service," a soft voice informed him.

"IP call, please, Security line. Balearic, 565-44-6019, in number thirty. Via laser; I don't want to wait all night for each answer."

There was a delay while she opened the line, and more delay after he tapped out a code. The face was not completely clear on the screen, but he recognized the man. "GunTek Interplanetary Corporation."

"Liquidation, please. Balearic, 565-44-6019, contract A-877. I mean B-877."

The man nodded and glanced aside. After a brief scanning of his records he said crisply, "Six operatives deceased. Your premium is now in category C, six-oh-one-nine."

"It seems a vutting shame that I have to credback your incompetence and inability to handle a simple contract," Balearic snapped.

GunTek shrugged. "We are not any happier with this situation than you. Our training isn't free, and we cannot afford such losses. We've never lost six men to one contractee before, either. Would you like to cancel?"

Roland sighed. "No. Premium category C, th—" He paused, noting a peculiar shifting in the man's eyes as the picture cleared, just for a moment. "*Do you know who you are?*"

"I think—" The man broke off, his features seeming to waver, not quite floating. Then his face firmed again. "Six operatives deceased. Your premium is now in category C, six-oh-one-nine."

"Accepted," Roland said quietly. "Connect me." And as the man nodded and the screen swam temporarily while he made the connection, Roland's smile faded.

°It's spreading! The continuum knows what's happening—Harmon is taking control!°

FIFTEEN...

"Vut," Chester grunted, and patted Lorna one last time. Monica grasped her hand and hurried her along the path away from the house. Lorna was flabbergasted, confused. It was all so casual. She had just stood there, while Chester held her, while Monica and the other boy had . . . just done it. Not until then had Monica asked where Randy might be.

Inside one of the lower level entrances, Monica ushered Lorna into a waiting elevator and said "Five." She grinned at Lorna, who was still staring.

"You just wait, Lorna. It's getting around. You're going to be a busy girl! Maybe you should consider a jay-girl career."

J-girl? But I'm . . . I was . . . I've been . . . yes, maybe I should . . .

They left the elevator, and she was conscious of the curious glances from the many strollers along the softly illuminated corridor. Of both sexes, the others ranged in color from light brown—Cauc mixture—to the inexpressibly beautiful purple-black of the few pure Afs left in the world. Lorna's feeling of conspicuous pallidity was magnified in the crowded hall, and she kept close to Monica. Monica still smelt like male.

She squeezed the smaller girl's hand in reassurance. "Relax, honey. None of them'll try to flash you unless

131

you say so. It's our biggest pastime in creche, but it's purely voluntary."

"Patricia—"

"Oh, be serious. Patricia's been wanting to be raped for at least a year. I kept telling Randy, but he wouldn't do it. He's . . . odd."

"Oh, *thanks*," Lorna said, then, in a tiny voice, "I'm not really worried about it, Monica, if you say so. It's just that I *stand out so*."

"Poor little girl." Monica kissed her cheek, a walking peck. "Just think, there used to be lots of people even paler than you! Just look at all the shades of brown and try to consider yourself the lightest shade, that's all." She waved a hand at the passersby. "Think of all the beautiful boys you're going to meet. You're lucky, you know? You're starting fresh. I've been through over half of them, because I grew up here. The repeats are dull, believe me, except with a few who really know what they're doing." She sighed. "One lesson last week indicated that's how we hold the population down, though, and everybody knows we don't want to go back to overpop." She shuddered. "It must have been awful, nearly four hundred million people just *in this country*!"

"How many are there?"

"What? How many—oh, boys?" Monica thought about it. "Between two hundred and thirty and two-forty, after the last Rites. There are about five hundred of us here, in all. But it changes all the time. You know—eight-year-olds leave the nurseries and come in, and twenty-year-olds Rite out." She sighed. "Those little ones can be a pain. Oh, well, I guess we're lucky to have such fertile mate-slaves. I heard that some of the other creches have facilities for a thousand, and less than two hundred kids. Must be funny, all that empty space."

The sound of weirdly electronic music reached their ears, and Monica grimaced. "That's Randoban! I tell him and *tell* him to keep the volume down so he won't disturb the others!"

"Who?"

"Randoban Kolumbu, the doll I want you to meet. I

know he's gentle; he's my brother. He also initiated me, years and *years* ago."

Monica was practically pulling Lorna along when they entered the concert hall. Like any normal human being, Lorna wanted to be an adult, but . . . They passed a listen-booth containing, snugly, two boys and a girl.

"Hey, Monnie! Can you put the quiets on your sib? You're the only one can break through his trance without a war club!"

"I'll take care of it," Monica promised. With Lorna close behind, she trotted down the line of supposedly soundproof booths and turned in to where a coal-black young man sat. His gleaming face wore an expression of deepest concentration. Monica sat down facing him, across his legs, and stuck wetted fingertips in both his ears. He jabbed at the sound button without looking. The booth was silent as he grabbed his sister.

"Easy sib, easy," Monica told him. "I want you to meet someone."

Randy looked up. His eyes started to widen, but stopped as his features opened in an engaging grin. Lorna felt the shivery feeling all along her spine. Monica's brother and choice for her was a doll. *What a contrast we'd make, with him so* black! *We'd be just beautiful!*

"Well, hello," he said. It was an amiable voice, well modulated, matching the relaxed self-assurance of finely, almost sharply chiseled features. "Pardon me, but what the voto are you doing in this creche?"

Monica tilted her head impishly. "Rather have a purple girl?" She laughed, swinging her legs on either side of his. "This's Lorna, Randy. My brother, Randoban. *I* didn't ask why she's here, because it's her own business and you *know* Gov doesn't do anything without a reason. She's also just been through a hospital—but she's not a regen, I mean she's not *old*. But guess what?"

"Uh . . . she used to be black?" He had a habit of cocking his head on one side.

Monica laughed. "The poor kid needs you, Randy. She's been revirginated and she's a little afraid. I've told her how gentle you are."

133

They both looked at Lorna. She stood still, flushed, like a slave at auction. A pretty little redheaded Cauc slave, in an Af creche. Smiling Monica took her hand and placed it in Randy's. His fingers gripped hers, strength without flagrant pressure.

"Hi."

"Hello."

"If—I can understand if . . . I'm sorry I'm so pale."

Randy grinned, beautiful flash of white teeth against black face. "White and beautiful," he said.

"Oh, come on," Monica said, "she's not *white!*"

"I'm sorry," Randy said, smiling easily again, or still, seeing Lorna's reaction to the sting of the word.

"That's that," Monica said, backing off his legs and stepping out of the booth. The two were gazing at each other, ignoring her. "Randy knows where our house is, so he'll bring you home. Have fun, kids." And she exited.

A thought surfaced in Lorna's mind: *the cruelty of adolescents.* Then it sank, like an iron meteorite. She was smiling bemazedly down at the contrast of her hand in his intensely black one; oh god, she *did* look so revoltingly *white!*

"You," he said easily, "are beautiful."

She stared. "You are." She looked down. "Does—does your sister always act like that?"

"No, she was almost human one day last year. I remember distinctly." He laughed. "You just brought out the shepherd in her . . . and the sibling empathy. You're the first new face over eight years old we've ever seen." He studied her. "You're also the absolutely cutest."

Only somewhat relaxed, she smiled her thanks. "What—what was that you were listening to?"

"Electrosonic vibrations on an interrelation of themes by Vivaldi and Beethoven, by Hiram Gosovobo," he said, and grinned at her blank look. "Some people think it's an esthetic monstrosity. I like it. It's . . . interesting. Exciting."

"Let's listen."

He nodded happily and drew her into the booth. The strange music welled up around them. It was, just as he'd

134

said, exciting. The booth became warm. Then it became smaller. Eventually, he closed the door. Eventually, she screamed, once. And she screamed again, six or seven minutes later. When they emerged in a disheveled glow from the booth, they were holding hands and smiling. They walked slowly to Monica's apartment. Lorna, of course, was sure she was in love.

The morning bell sounded softly through the house, and Monica opened her eyes, yawning. For a moment she stared at the pale girl who lay indecorously in her bed. Then she nodded, smiled, and ran her fingers through Lorna's soft hair. "Hey, wake up, red. They won't call you for breakfast a second time."

Lorna opened her eyes sleepily, then frowned, glancing confusedly about. The blank look left her eyes when she turned to Monica. "Oh, hi, Monnie." She stretched luxuriously. "Ummm. I feel so *good*."

Monica laughed, told her to come shower, and ran. Lorna followed, less alacritously. Monica handed her a shower cap and teased her with words and touches while they showered. After drying, they went into the other room to work on their hair.

"What are you studying, Monica?"

"Good question! I've been getting the standard general sauce for years: history, math, lit, sociology, general and personal; all the things they think we should know. Some elemental psych, lately. I came into the classroom one morning and found a simple layout for biological experiments, and a reprogrammed machine."

Lorna examined the strand of hair she drew out of Monica's comb. "That must've been confusing. What do you think they have in mind?"

"Medicine?" Monica shrugged. "When Gov decides on educational direction, they work it in slowly, so they can change it if it doesn't work out. They're usually right. Anyhow, I now have a little assortment of chemicals and exodermics. I had to use them on small animals and report to the teaching machine. They're still tossing it at me.

Maybe there's medicine in my future." She chuckled. "They sure fouled up Randy."

"Oh, they *wouldn't!*" Lorna stopped combing. "What did they do?"

Monica grinned at her. "Monnie's always right. Fell just like that, didn't you? I'll have to make sure you get some variety. Well, he thought he was going music, but that brought out his math faculty. Before he knew what was happening, he was being eased into celestial navigation."

"Wow! *Why?*"

"They need him, and that's where his mind seems to lean. He doesn't have to go with the fleet. After Rites, the choice is his. But it isn't bothering him; navigational curves fascinate him as much as human ones . . . or music. There's a connection, you know." She dropped her comb on the dresser. "You almost ready?"

"Ready," Lorna said, and they donned sandals and went down to eat.

Lorna's day was her own after breakfast. Until the records were checked, she could not be assigned classes in any particular direction. She idled away the time by attending a class with Monica, strolling about the creche, familiarizing herself with the grounds. That night it was Randy again; they both preferred it. And sleep, and another morning, and another night: Pete Naseembanu had given her a lot of attention, and he gave a lot of attention to ecstatting her. But she thought of Randy.

Subtle alterations insinuated themselves into her psychological structure as more days passed. Her past burrowed deeper into her subconscious. Gradually, her mind erected its barrier against memory, without scarring her. The creche and the people in it became her world.

She was waiting when Randy stepped out of his study room. It had become such a normal procedure that no one showed surprise, nor did Randy. Lorna blended naturally into his embrace, her lips meeting his in mutual acceptance of the complete normality of their preference for each other. Each with an arm around the other, they

136

walked to the elevator, sublimely oblivious of others. The elevator surfaced them, and they moved to the outer door.

Randy glanced at the sky. He held a hand outside. "Raining." He looked down at her with a smile. "Shall we go back Under or take a walk in the rain?"

Lorna caressed the hand on her waist. "The rain can't hurt people without clothes."

Laughing, he grasped her hand and stepped outside. Droplets pelted them, slicking down their bare bodies. Their steps quickened as the cool water exhilarated them. Then the rain increased, pouring in rivulets from them. They ran laughing down the path.

Randy stopped suddenly. He pulled Lorna close, looking down into her wet-glistening face. "I know a secret place where *nobody* goes. It's not far—and there's not much grass, just trees and privacy. Want to see it?"

She squeezed him close. "Of course!"

She felt as people must have felt in the far, far past, running naked through lovely verdure with the rain sluicing down over her bare body, to find a secret place just for her and her lover. She was happy in the creche; it was the beginning of a new world.

IV: END OF THE BEGINNING

Before the Survivor "died," he knew what he had begun.

The prisms—projected gene-patterns of electronic origin —he had imprinted on the aborigines *were* the aborigines. Their mating created new gene-combinations. Each became an independent entity, but they were still only identity archetypes, not human offspring, and they possessed no genetic potential. But they added a new factor to Probability. They formed continua, in separate directions, without losing contact with those interrelated generations— that, slowly, fanned out in a chain reaction. To infinity.

The race could have progressed in any of many directions. Because of the oddity of genesis, there was always potential for contact between lines of probability. That factor should have presented no problem.

But the Survivor changed all that, unknowingly.

He mated with the "reincarnation" of his sister. She became a/the secondary pattern. When their offspring intermated with the others, a Prime pattern emerged: the only genuine pattern.

With only a nascent concept of the result of his coition, the Survivor reached the end of his long life. He "died." And lived on, over and over and ever and ever. Like an amoeba in its endless and helpless cycle, the continuum separated and reseparated into an infinite number of variants. Prime dominated; the Survivor, as the only true human, dominated the race, the entire continuum. It accepted that dominance without question. The continuum was the domain of the Prime(s). They continued to exist, always, as sentient life, whether they reincarnated or not.

With the passage of eons came dilution. But now and again the pure strain emerged: when it was perfect, Prime Maximus existed, in both a male and a female manifestation. Both were aware of their genetic distribution throughout the race; whatever part of the race experienced, Maximus knew/felt.

Sometimes centuries passed without contact between the male and female Prime Maximus. Their bodies might be married, without their ever surfacing. They lived as normal human beings, submerged in the carriers' subconsciouses. Basically they were just that: their powers were limited to connection with the entire genetic continuum and the ability to manipulate it if necessary. They could make contact with others of their kind across probability lines, and thus with each other via feedback: a sort of roundabout telepathy.

Man's leaving Earth and establishing himself on Mars and Venus raised complications, perhaps separating the male and female Primes. So did the existence of the Others, who were to become the Antagonist.

Some prisms remained behind when the Survivor escaped the doomed worlds. The sole purpose of those imprinted gene-codes was the transmission of identity. Remaining behind on the fragments of the destroyed planet, they were submitted to the vacuum, and they became transmitters of the energy they carried. Their probability patterns were minimal, their universe linear. There was no Prime Maximus among them, for there was but one *human* Survivor.

And then there was 944 Hidalgo, recognized as early as 1920 as . . . eccentric. Two astronomical units from Sol at perihelion, it swept out to nine-and-a-half AU at aphelion, near Saturn's orbit. And it was inclined forty-three degrees, a cometary orbit. But it had no nebulosity, and so was not a comet, merely . . . odd. And man, his population problem solved and his life easy and rather hedonistic, did not bother to go farther out—with one exception—than Mars. Hidalgo remained an enigma. And the Antagonist found it.

And then there were Wesley Harmon, and Lorna who had not been his sister but who was now, and Harriet and Roland Balearic (Roland plus Balearic), and Tommy, and he who was both Prime and an agent for the Antagonist, and the decoy, and . . . Prime Maximus.

Distance is only the measure of the movement of an object through time.

Time is only the measure of the distance involved in an object's movement.

Cogimus, ergo sumus . . . cogimus!

SIXTEEN...

The Martian cabby, whose lineage appeared to have been mostly Cauc plus Mong, nodded at the narrow entranceway flanked by extruglass bricks.

"That's the place," he said. "Nice section, huh?" He grinned. "But Tommy's is a lezbar, and Tommy is an Af citizen. Maybe she can help you find your Harriet. But— big as you are, I wouldn't be one bit surprised to see you come flying out of there on your ass. Keep your gun loose."

Wes nodded, paid him off with the cash Martians doted on, and climbed out. He did not even glance back as the taxi gunned off. A tension was building in the stream of his psyche. Something was tugging at his senses like a magnet, calling like the wraith of a whisper. Hardly conscious of motion, he was advancing through a sea of psychological waves that flowed through the ever-widening door of his comprehension.

He opened the door and stepped through. His eyes searched through the dimly lit room; his ears strove to sort out the babble of feminine voices. They seemed to surge around him, vaporizing as his concentration centered on the one voice that rang in his mind like an alarm.

Then he saw the eyes, bright in the dark face that stared at him from across the room in instant recognition.

140

He caught the glint of light on metal, and his own hand shot into his jac to pluck out his own gun.

The room was filled with a sudden torrent of brilliant light as space and time flowed and writhed around him. He heard the thunder of a tortured world. *She* was suddenly there, jet black hair whipping in the winds of devastation, red robes swirling in madness as she glided from him. Her body touched that of the big brown woman. It seemed to waver. Then their figures seemed to blend in undulating fusion as her eyes widened in astonishment.

Tongues of flame stabbed from Harriet's gun. Solid-fueled missiles slammed into the wall behind Harmon. Directly behind him. His own gun was out, but the place was in such a seething uproar that sighting on her was impossible.

Her smoking gun was empty. Her dumbfounded eyes stared at him, the big man standing there unharmed. Her cry was a throaty grunt. Stumbling into the throng of screaming lesbies, she flowed with them toward a side exit, knowing she had to escape—

(into the endless roads of time and find the)

slipping the dressing gown from her shoulders and smiling up at him in glowing anticipation

(through the howling winds of eternity that flowed toward the)

so many lonely years. No man can satisfy me because they just don't know how and I can't show them

gazing at the wall with unseeing eyes as he pulled at the narcostic

—(stream of remembrance that led to the garden)—the garden! "The garden!" Harriet screamed, whirling in the maelstrom of panicky women.

Wes held his fire in frustration, watching the mob surge into the exit. The woman of the flames had vanished; had he been the only person here who had seen her? He backed against the wall—

slipping the sonoknife from under the bar and moving swiftly toward the big man holding the gun

—and glanced quickly to his right, centering the deadly muzzle of his .45 on the woman coming at him with the

141

naked blade. She stopped short, glaring at him. Her prettiness astonished him. She looked familiar, too.

She tossed the knife to the floor. "Okay, scumbum, I can't top that gun. What's the idea coming in here and causing all this hell?"

Wes smiled with deliberate lack of concern. "No smoke coming from this gun, Tommy. It all came from Harriet's." He waggled the pistol. "Where's she likely to have gone?"

Tommy folded her arms beneath her breasts, her old-gold face almost without expression. "You think I'm going to tell *you* about a lesbie, jacko, you're fobby." She tilted her head back to attack him with a short, scornful laugh. "I think you're buggy, anyhow."

"More than you think," he assured her. He backed up to slam and lock the front door, then waved his gun toward the rear of the empty room. "Start walking." He detoured to secure the side exit.

She shrugged, turned, and strolled back through the overturned chairs and tables. She hesitated only long enough to step on a smoldering cigaret and grind it out. "What have you got on your alleged mind, bigshot?"

"Information," he told her, following her down the narrow hallway. He motioned her to one side at the far end, while he made sure the door was locked. "All I want is some scrute about Harriet. I think you can tell me, and you're going to, citizen." He glanced along the door lining the hall. "Which is your apartment?"

She eyed him insolently for a moment; contempt was the only weapon left to a woman faced by a lamentably big man with a lamentably big gun. Even without the pistol, he appeared capable of breaking her in two.

"You'd find it anyhow," she muttered, and opened one of the doors. "My apt. You're not invited—" She jerked her spine very straight when he prodded her with the muzzle of the revolver. "All right, all right, *Entrez*."

First glancing past her to be certain the room was empty, he pushed her inside and closed the door. Across the comfortable-looking room was another doorway; part of a bed was visible. He let her feel the gun again. "Into the bedroom."

"Now wait a minute, paisano—"

"Into the bedroom." He prodded lower on her back, and she quivered exasperatedly, then hurried into her bedroom. She turned angrily. "What in hell are you going to do?"

He gazed at her. Pretty; angular face, cheekbones and chin as though hand-carved by a perfectionist. Close-cropped black hair with hints of very dark red in it, raggedly banked across her forehead. Ultra-thin gold rings in her pierced ears. She was very slim, wearing a sand-ochre tunic, loose and loosely belted, and black pants that looked sprayed on. And bare feet, no paler than her face, which was about the color of a new penny.

"What'm I going to do? Get the truth out of a very pretty lesbie. Peel."

Her eyes flared. "*No!*"

"Tommy, I don't think I'll shoot you, not really. But I swear I'll use the gun on you, one way or another." He strove to look mean.

"You . . . son of a *bitch*." She whispered it, staring, quivering, watching the gun rise to stare back at her from its single dark eye. She raised her angry eyes to his, and she held them there while she peeled.

He glanced around, backed to her closet, and opened it. He ran his hand through the dangling garments until he found a robe. Pulling the cord out, he returned to her. "Turn around and put your hands back."

"Look, jacko, for godsake—all this just for Harriet?"

She winced as he pulled it tightly about her wrists, and she cried out in surprise: a blow across the back of her knees drained the strength from her legs. She dropped. A big hand clamped her head, fingers curling into her hair. Still on her knees, she was forced to hobble over to the bed. "Bastard!"

He sat on the edge of the bed facing the kneeling girl, watching her struggle in futile outrage. "Come on, Tommy. Where'd Harriet go?"

"How should I know? She's just one of hundreds that come in here regular. She—" She broke off, watching his hand drop to the hem of his klamys. Suddenly realizing

143

what he intended, she jerked her head out of his grasp. "*No*! You're not going to do it! You *cant*! Not to ME!"

He shrugged. "Tell me about Harriet, little woman."

"Damn you—"

He didn't bother to argue. He did it to her, holding tightly to her head with one hand and making sure she saw the gun in the other. He did his best to scare her into believing he intended strangling her. And he was amazed, several gasping minutes later, at her long sigh. Slowly, she relaxed. Her shoulders slumped, began to shudder. He tilted her face up again. She was sobbing, shaking with the sobs. Tears flowed down her face.

"You son of a bitch," she said very quietly, without emphasis or enthusiasm, as though she were drugged. "You did it—and you made me like it. I hate you. I *hate* you."

He lifted her easily and placed her, still bound, on her own bed. She wriggled around to bury her face in the pillow.

°*so many lonely years. No man can satisfy me because they just don't know and I can't show them*°

°*I can*°

She jerked her head back to stare at him with wide eyes.

"You—you have it, too! You . . . *heard* me!"

He nodded, sitting down to put a hand on her shoulder. "In the head. And you heard me?"

She nodded. "My god, I've been hearing it for *years*. It's driven me half out of my mind. Do you have any idea of the *thoughts* in a man's mind when he starts to—" She shuddered. "Just an object, a hole to be filled. No one of them could satisfy me . . . they just disgusted me. And I couldn't tell them or show them how—" Her eyes swam in a glistening pool of tears.

"So it became women."

She nodded against the pillow. "Yes. So it became women."

"Here," he said, "wiggle around and let me get you untied, Tommy."

"You're not going to *leave*!"

144

He couldn't be that cruel . . .
I'm not that cruel.

"No," he told her, but she had already heard him and was reaching for him.

SEVENTEEN...

After dinner Lorna sat on the front steps to watch the evening sun die in orange splendor. It reminded her— everything did—of the inevitable loss of Randy, and her eyes moistened. She was hardly aware that someone had sat beside her until Monica spoke.

"Beautiful sunset."

Lorna sniffled.

Monica looked at her in surprise, then slipped an arm around her shoulders. "Baby! What're you crying about?"

Lorna let the tears flow unrestrained. "I'm going to lose Randy in six months when they put him in pre-Rites."

"Honey, honey, it's not that bad." Monica patted her shoulder. "You'll be seeing him again. Why, you'll probably be out of here before he is."

"Me?" Lorna blinked wet lashes. "I'm only sixteen."

"Sure, but they'll release you as soon as they see your sponsor papers."

Lorna looked uncomprehendingly at her. "Sponsor papers?"

"Sure, you know. You told me—Lorna?" The smile left her lips as her mind assimilated Lorna's plaintive query. She touched the girl's cheek, turning her head so that their eyes met. "Lorna? Don't you remember your sponsor?"

The eyes gazed back at her with blank ingenuousness.

146

Monica's alert mind raced. "Lorna : . . do you remember the . . . outside?"

Lorna shook her head vaguely. "I've been here all the time."

Monica was speechless. Holding her arm around the girl's shoulders with gentle firmness, she frowned, trying to sort it out. Her voice was nervous even after she cleared her throat.

"Lorna—you know this is an Af creche, don't you?"

"Of course, Monnie. That's why we're all here."

Trying to keep her hand from shaking, Monica laid it on Lorna's thigh in sharp contrast. "Kitten, don't you think you're a little light of skin for an Af?"

"Uh-huh. I know my skin's lighter than anybody else's, but nobody pays any attention. Randy loves me, anyway." Lorna looked nervously at the other girl. "It doesn't bother you, does it, Monnie?"

Monica kissed her quickly on the forehead. "No, of course not. We're like sisters." *Good god*, she thought *she thinks she's an Af! There's no way to tell her different . . . she's the only Cauc here!* Ordinarily, what Lorna thought would make no difference; the separate creches were established by the League only as a recognition of national sovereignty, and Africans were more uptight about racial dilution than the rest of the world. But Lorna's case indicated some form of amnesia. Why? Randy couldn't have caused it, surely. The more she thought about Lorna, the more mysterious Monica realized the girl's coming here was. Something was radically wrong, hidden deep within the girl's mind. What if the attendants learned she'd forgotten her past? How would the other kids react? And Gov—

Monica's heartbeat quickened. She dared allow herself to consider the things she'd been studying, the vials and exodermic syringes she now possessed . . . it couldn't hurt Lorna . . . and it might keep both her and Randy out of a mess of some sort if he were involved in her amnesia. . . .

"Honey, you're mostly tired. Why don't you come over with me tonight and I'll read to you."

147

Strangely, dreamily tractable, Lorna allowed herself to be persuaded, and ten minutes later she was gazing at the sonolight as Monica read aloud, and within twenty minutes more Lorna was deep in a hypnotic sleep. Monica read furiously, double-checked everything, and then held the exodermic against the girl's arm and juiced the polyscopotetrolanide into her veins.

The skinny boy leaned out of the vizbooth and yelled down the hall, "Randy still here?"

"RANDY!"

Randy appeared at the head of the stairs. "What is is?"

"Monica's on the viz; says it's urgent."

Randy trotted down to the booth quickly as the other boy edged out. Randy closed the door.

Monica's smile vanished when she saw him. "I'm in my room. Get over here as fast as you can."

"What's the rush? We were going to play—"

"Randy, Lorna's here asleep and there's something on the tape you've *got* to hear."

"Sib, I'm not interested in who she does what with. We—"

"Randy, it isn't that, and get over here quick." Monica blanked the screen, which was a guarantee that he would run all the way. He did.

Lorna didn't waken when he burst into the room. She seemed all right, although he noticed the sheet was wet with perspiration. Then Monica started the tape, and he heard Lorna's voice, and Monica's, quietly asking questions, and then Lorna's, changing, changing . . . and they listened, staring at each other.

When the tape had ended and Monica shut it off, Randoban Kolumbu stared silently at the Cauc girl on the sweaty sheets. He shook his head slowly. "What a hell of a thing to happen."

"What do we do?" Monica asked. "It isn't just a simple case of her believing she's an Af."

Randy started to reply, then rose and went to Lorna as she stirred. He sat beside her, lifting her and holding her close, her head on his shoulder. His face was suddenly older as he looked at his sister.

"Sib, this is still my girl. I don't care what she used to be."

"She's your girl whether she has a past or not, Randy. That's your kid she's growing in her belly."

"What makes you so sure she's pregnant?"

"Vut, Randy, you heard the tape!" Monica leaned back against the table where the recorder sat, black and abruptly ugly. "I pulled all that stuff out of her subcon. That's real memory, sib. Since her regeneration, she has a double mens, and she had her last period a week before she came here. She's had time for plenty more—and she's had none. It's partly my fault. I introduced you the first night she came."

"You . . . couldn't have known. . . ."

"No, dammit." She chewed her lip, counting the tiles on the floor. Her head jerked up. "Does it bother you? knowing she's nine years older than you are?"

He touched Lorna's cheek. "She's sixteen. That's all. Sixteen, and my girl. The question is whether it's going to bother *her*. How in the vutting hell did her mind blank out like that?"

Monica hoisted her brows. "That's obvious enough. She had an experience no one would wish on anyone. It should have driven her completely buggo. They saved her mind and her body both, by regeneration and metabolic rectification, and psyconditioning. They were trying to stabilize her at this age level without loss of identity, I can see that. When the police picked her up, they lost control of the conditioning pattern. She became just a kid looking for a haven, a safe place." She sighed, walking over to glance up at the sky, then swinging back to face him. "You and me and the creche represent protection, personal and tangible, Randy, and she grabbed at it. The memories nosedived into her subcon. They were too horrible to keep. That girl you're holding is the beginning of an altogether different woman."

"A mateslave," he murmured. "As soon as they learn she's preg, that's what she'll be. A mateslave. She'll have to be; anyone else who has babies is performing an illegal act. And to make it a complete paradox, she's too young to be punished."

"And to make a mess of it," she pointed out, "you're heading into pre-Rites in six months. Randy, by the time she's through all of it, she'll be an irretrievable bug." She fiddled with the dials of her teaching machine. "Randy . . . so far as the world is concerned, this girl doesn't *exist*. Sib . . . how much do you love her?"

He held Lorna close, his hands tight. "You know! Why?"

"I'm thinking this is too dangerous even to try an abortion. But—you could run away with her."

He stared at her, then laughed bitterly. "Where to? The Congo jungle reserve? We'd *both* go buggy among the aborigines!"

"Randy, you aren't thinking. Your sights are too low." She smiled confidently. "There's another place."

"I really think this ain't the time to play enigmatic games, sib, do you. Anybody can locate anybody in this world. There's no place on Earth . . . you're thinking of *Callisto!*"

"Now you've got it," she grinned. "Why not?"

"For starts, how do we get there, on roller skates?"

"No, dear brother, by spaceship. One call home from me—that's all it would take. *All*, Randy. And you *can* handle one, can't you?"

"Probably. But—"

"But do you know what you'll be getting into? What do you know about Callisto?"

He scratched his nose. "It's a male dream. It's Comstock's Planet now. Captain Comstock was the man sent out there to check out the radio broadcasts. What he found was evidence of an ancient civilization: prime evidence, like a whole damned terraformed planet run by a computer. The computer's job was to wait for a master—and it decided Comstock was it. It also proved it could vaporize any ship that got anywhere near close, and Gov and the League ceded Callisto to Comstock." Randy grinned. "With him were one black man and two women. They called him traitor till he sent back the ore samples, and the tapes. The samples were richer than anything on the three planets. The tape contained the voice of one of the richest women in the System. She became his mateslave—voluntarily. And—well, sure I know. Since then maybe a hundred couples, mavericks, have gone out there for sanctuary from the mateslave laws. Comstock says his planet has the only *real* Freewill in the system. And no one argues, because of the trade. They still call him evil, though, him and his harem."

Monica stored away the recorder before turning and saying, "Sometimes evil's just a matter of what's different from what you've been taught. Maybe we don't know the whole story about mateslaves. Maybe *it's* evil."

"Monica!"

She laughed. "Come on, think straight human instead of male. What do we know? The mateslave-Freewill system's been with us a long time, and yes, I know what things were like before. Accidental breeding—" she shivered. And suddenly her eyes widened as she stared at the girl he held.

"Yes," he whispered. "Like us."

Monica nodded, wide-eyed. "Well . . . our life expectancy's up over two hundred years and getting higher with each new regen discovery. Imagine what would happen with uncontrolled birth and no place to go."

Randy eyed her thoughtfully. "All right. I'll admit that *may* justify the slavery. Not all women can stand it, even if they do think they want to reproduce."

"Right. Only those who consider it the most important thing in their lives—atavists. Can you think of a better way to keep out those females who'd just do it as a lark? That's the way some of the women were in the old 'marriage' days." She wandered nervously, her brow rumpled as she concentrated on new thoughts. "Think about it—we hold mateslaves up to the most brutal contempt—but give them the very finest of care. It's a contradic—well." She turned and sat down suddenly. "We're getting away from the main subject, Randy."

"You ready to make that call?"

"Oh, brother, brother . . . I don't want you to go . . . yes. I'm ready to make the call. But you know what you'll have to do. Just clear out. I'll cover for you while you grab the ship. Just get the vut off Earth as fast as you can move!"

Staring at her, Randy tightened his arms again as Lorna moaned softly, moving. "Just like that. Without any preparations."

His sister nodded. "The faster you move, the fewer clues you leave, and the more confusion you'll create. We just—"

"Monnie . . . Randy?" Lorna was opening her eyes.

"Don't tell her all of it," Monica snapped, hurrying over to sit down beside them. "Hi, honey. I've got news. I know why you were feeling so funny. I called Randy over."

Lorna yawned and snuggled closer to him. "I can't think of a nicer way to wake u—found out what?"

"You—uh . . . hell, blurt it out," Monica told herself. "You're going to have a baby, that's what."

Lorna looked confused, then scared, then shamelessly delighted. She twisted her neck to kiss Randy. "Oh, *Randy*! I'm so happy."

Monica sighed, shaking her head. *She's forgotten all the rules; she doesn't even know it's a crime.* She stood up and leaned a firm hand on Lorna's shoulder.

"All right, Lorna, that doesn't bother you; good. I hope this won't, either. Randy is . . . going to have to take you far away. To another planet. A satellite of Jupiter's . . . Callisto."

Lorna was frowning. "I . . . think I've . . ." She looked at Randy. "I've heard of it, haven't I? We'll have to go there, won't we. I mean—we can't have a baby here. I'm too young . . . but . . . do you want—"

"Make that call, sib," Randy said, squeezing Lorna tightly.

Monica nodded with a bright smile, but she was weeping when she ran down to the other end of the hall to call home to Gambia.

It was so easy Randy wondered about god after all.

Maybe there was a paternal Overseer somewhere—where was heaven, now that the sky was only one more doorway? —who arranged things, and who had some special reason for making it simple for Randy, Lorna, and Monica to leave the creche with the representatives from Gambia; who hurled them at Monica when she began to vamp them, right there in the private lounge on the spacefield; who kept them very very busy with the girl, even while she and her brother exchanged one last look.

Then he and Lorna ran like hell, and still it was easy. The airlock stood open. He lifted her inside, activated the closing mechanism, and secured the inner lock. He led the shivering Lorna down the small passageway to the Doctor. She lay quietly, staring at him with huge eyes while he strapped her in.

"Sure, I know you don't need the Doctor," he grinned. "It's just a good place for you to be during acceleration." He bent to kiss her. "Trust Randy, sweetheart."

His heart felt as though someone had kicked it when she said softly, "Always."

Hurrying back to the pilot's compartment, he sat down to stare nervously at the control board. Cocking his head, he surveyed the elaborate instruments and dials with a rising feeling of dismay. "Oh, god! I never realized how complicated the real thing would be." Frantically, he strove to recall all he had learned from the simulator . . .

. . . *his boots echoing hollowly in the empty ship as he strode back to the control cabin, grimly accepting possession of the vessel after Manuel's hideous death. He examined the instrument panel with easy familiarity, mentally tracing every connection to its functional contact* . . .

. . . and grinned, reaching with complete confidence for the controls laughing silently about his stupid doubts about such a simple array of electronic equipment. He put aside doubts about the ship's ability to carry him and Lorna to their far destination. His fingers moved rapidly over the complex instruments. The ship came alive.

"Control to Gambia oh-nine-eight-oh! What the vutting sauce are you idiots doing out there?"

"Leaving," Randy said firmly. "Now. You'd better make

153

certain I'm clear, jacko, or the government of Gambia will be mighty damned mad at you and Gov!"

And while Control alternated yelling at him with bawling for help and arranging clearance, Randy took her up. Around . . . and around . . . and then out, out, becoming a steadily diminishing point of light that vanished against the starry background.

EIGHTEEN...

While Tommy ran into the bathroom, Wes lay back, gazing up at the ceiling. After traveling all that time through space, he could surely spend a few days with the woman obviously meant for him, as though there were indeed a Master Control somewhere arranging the affairs of men. He wasn't sure why the urge to reach the purveyors of the Star Pearls had lessened, but he knew it would come back. He was being led, driven, he was sure of that, pleasant or not. A swift and careful probe of Tommy's mind indicated nothing but delight. There was no animosity there, from the way he'd introduced them. He had to smile at what he did find there, and he tossed in a few ideas of his own. He heard her giggle.

A deep probe was out of the question. Her past was her own affair. Besides, he had no intention of letting anyone —not even Tommy, yet—know all he was capable of.

When she moved from the bathroom to her kitchen, he showered and began to dress.

"Please don't do that." He turned to see her in the kitchen doorway, wearing absolutely nothing. She smiled. "I like you naked."

"So do I. But it's customary for civilized people to wear clothing."

°*Don't lecture me, brain partner,*° she shot the thought at him as she came swiftly over to press warmly against him. °*We make our own civilization.*°

"After all," she said aloud, "we were naked in the creche. Certainly that was civilized. We don't need anything or anyone from the outside, Wes. The foodster's stocked, the telly's the latest, every door's locked, and surely *nobody* ever had more drinkables on hand. We have a private world, love."

Wes kissed her lips, very warm and soft, and ran his hands over the equally warm, equally smooth expanse of her bare back. He chuckled.

"In other words, a two-people orgy. Okay, love. You win—but let's eat."

They ate, hardly daring to look away from each other. They freed little snatches of thought from time to time, occasionally laughing aloud.

"Anybody saw us would think we're totally bugged out," he said.

"Nobody's looking, darling. Nobody. Wes . . . why do you want to kill Harriet?"

"Harriet wants to kill me. She tried to, on Earth. She had others try to. She and her . . . partner did things to my sister you wouldn't believe . . . probably to smash me. It didn't work."

She watched him, waiting, her brows up.

He sighed. "All right. For starts, I was a pimp. Shocked?"

She chuckled. "For starts, I was lesbie. Shocked?"

Wesley raised a hand in salute. "All right. I represented my sisters, and what Harriet and somebody named Balearic did to one of them is why I came here. And yes, I intend to kill them. I have to."

"Wes? I'd never suspect Harriet of anything like that. Are you sure it was she?"

"Not completely," he admitted, patting his naked chest for cigarets before he realized that all he wore was the napkin draped across his thighs. He grinned when she ran for his cigarets, grinned again when she snatched the napkin. He swatted her as she returned to her chair.

"Harriet was connected, though. She set it up, and she called me, after. To be sure I knew they'd done it. I think I understand why they did it, but there's no sense

156

going into that." He exhaled a slow dribble of smoke and watched it snake ceilingward. "Don't worry about it. But be ready for me to leave in a few days. I *have* to follow her. Where'd she go, Tommy?"

"Oh, Wes, I have more reason for not telling you now than before!"

He nodded, keeping his eyes on hers. She sighed. "She was having a fling before she left for Hidalgo, wherever that is. She—"

"I know where it is," he said—

(*raising the neutron rifle, Maximus pressed the trigger and a ravening stream of energy lashed out*)

Tommy set the drinks on the bar and came around to take the stool beside him. They touched glasses and sipped the cold liquid, peering at each other over the tops of the tumblers. "Is it all right?"

"It's perfect. Ever consider opening a bar, lady?"

She chuckled, glancing down the empty café to the curtained door. The room was lit pallidly by the daylight that crept through the extruded glass bricks. They could hear the traffic outside, faintly. She laughed.

"I wonder what they'd think out there if they knew there was a naked man and woman sitting in here at the bar."

He smiled, reaching to caress her bare shoulder. They'd envy us, Tommy."

"Wes? You know what? I love you."

He nodded. "Of course. Someone created us that way, darling."

"But what would they *think*?" she asked, grinning and waving a hand at the door.

He shrugged. "Can't imagine. What d'you imagine they'd think if they knew the owner of this place was about to be laid on her own bar?"

Her grin widened, as his did.

Roland Balearic, alone in his room, sat staring at an undecorated wall. His eyes did not blink. He did not speak; he was too busy making his report.

°Balearic persona reporting. I remain in complete control. No one thinks my actions are any more peculiar than usual, although I must admit that this Balearic manifestation is a pain. I feel as though I have a split personality with delirium trimmings. Currently I am manipulating a total of five personae—six, including this Balearic thing. The Harmon persona continues to maintain its block, naturally. Since he is a genetic Prime, the entire continuum is at his disposal—you, me, everyone. Corland—you are the end of the continuum, aren't you?°

And Corland's answer flowed into his mind, tinged with amusement:

°You're trying to trap me into a positive answer for your own peace of mind, Balearic. No. I am not the end of the continuum. So far as I am aware, the only established limit in *any* direction is . . . Harmon. I, too, am being coordinated; I am a Prime *persona*, as you are.°

°And you are coordinating me, and I am coordinating Harmon. Glad it stops somewhere! I might wind up praying. How many variants do *I* have?°

°You know I can't give you that information, Balearic. Most of them are in neutral positions, anyhow. The ones you're using are all you really need. Let's get on with the report. You're having no pattern interference problem? I can initiate stronger blocks if you need them. Oh—I also understand your situation. But the continuum had no way of anticipating such a condition as the shattering of a Prime Maximus pattern! You were the only remaining stable persona, and that left you open to control by the Antagonist. You're doing very well, Balearic—for a prisoner.°

°Yes . . . with Harmon as the key to my cell. I can't extricate from this . . . mess, until he reaches Contact Point. And I can't reach CP until he stabilizes the Prime variant. Lorna₁ has been diverted; the Harmon persona was too strong, and would only have resulted in confusion. Fortunately, the Antagonist considered it a necessary move in eliminating interference from Harmon, and cooperated in . . . what I did to her. I did everything possible to convince the Antagonist it would do no good, but

158

they won't and can't realize how different this universe is from theirs. They can't understand that they are patterns *only*, that we have Primes. Scientific logic can sometimes be positively . . . absurd.°

Derision. °How existential! Lorna$_2$?°

°—is progressing nicely, but she doesn't know who/ what she is, yet—because I am blocking. That's necessary until I've coordinated Harmon and Lorna$_3$; her being on a different planet certainly complicated this operation! At any rate, Three is the stabilization persona. I think you can understand what a delicate problem *that* is—like juggling a bomb.°

°A time bomb, yes. Proceed. The generator Harmon is carrying?°

Balearic's face did not change, but he mentalized mild apprehension. °It's behaving remarkably well. I have no contact with the Antagonist that initiated it, but I believe they think *they* activated Harmon, by projecting it into his presence. They didn't, of course; Prime Maximus knew everything the moment I was trapped. He merely had not surfaced to Harmon's conscious level. They're using his generator's affinity with the continuum as a homing signal, to invade this universe. Again, they can't conceive of how complicated this universe is. They assume it's a linear pattern, like theirs.°

°They're in for a surprise!°

°Yes . . . oh yes, Corland, there was a bit of difficulty. Lorna$_2$ was nearly fully incarnated by the feedback, but I managed to block it in time. Now she's wondering at her own strangeness. *She* is the Prime persona in this part of the conflict; it's she who must split their continuum. She may not survive incarnate, any more than I will. The real problem is that she'll be highly charged, and might incarnate rapidly as a composite.°

Unconcern from Corland: °We'll assist in setting up the necessary blocks against that. Did you clarify Arcturus Four?°

°Not yet. It doesn't exist in the Antagonist's continuum, so they have no knowledge of it. I'll go out for a look when they break through. I'll use their time factor as a bypass, and it'll take only a few seconds on their energy output. But from what I gathered on first penetration, it's some two thousand years from now.°

°It has to be related to this continuum, Balearic. You'd have detected it, otherwise. We'll maintain contact and be available the moment Harmon completes the cycle. Understood?°

°Understood. Bring a headache remedy. *That* will be an uncomfortable moment.°

°It will be far more uncomfortable for the Antagonist. They won't try to incorporate us into their conflicts again, Balearic.°

°*If* there is any "again" for them, after Harriet splits their continuum. She's approaching Troy now.°

Harmon (scanned the planet and detected the blind spot on the outskirts of Troy. It vanished; he knew where it was going. Delicately, he probed the Harriet pattern, then withdrew. Tomorrow the trail would begin again, but for now he) enjoyed the warmth of Tommy's body against his as she slept in his arms.

He awoke to the Martian daylight hazing dimly through the curtained windows. He caressed the woman's soft brown skin and kissed her gently. "Time to wake up, Tommy. The party's over."

She rolled over onto her back, sighing sleepily. Then she cuddled warmly back against him. "It can't be. We just started."

"It is," he chuckled. "We've been drilling and cooing for three days—screwing and wooing, they used to call it. It's time to wake up to the woes of the contin—the universe. You have to open the bar, and I have to be on my way. I have a schedule to keep."

She jerked around and sat up to look down at him, curious. "What kind of schedule? Is that what you're hiding from me?"

He reached up to squeeze one bare breast gently. "Can't tell you, kitten. Besides, you're not supposed to know I'm hiding something from you."

She leaned down quickly to kiss him before speaking

softly with her eyes an inch from his. "We're both hiding something from everyone, darling, and that's the very reason we'll have a hard time keeping secrets from each other. But it isn't a woman, and you aren't a criminal. So I won't ask or peep, until you're ready to tell me." She swung her feet to the floor and stood up, entertaining him by inhaling deeply and running her hands over herself. She smiled wickedly at him.

"Just don't forget where I am when you're finished. Three days isn't enough for what we can do, doll. We need years and years!" She started kitchenward, flinging back over her shoulder. "Take a shower and check your god-awful gun. I'll drive you to the field when I've fed you."

She did, and less than two hours later she dropped her car down before the gate leading to his berthed ship. She cut the engine and turned disconsolately to him. "I won't get out with you. This is bad enough as it is."

"Don't worry, Tommybabe. I'll be back and we'll pick up right where we left off."

"I wish I could be sure of that, Wes."

He shot her a look into his mind that should have been reassuring, then told her, "Tommy, I can't tell you everything because I don't know all of it. But I can tell you one nice little item: I can't be killed. I'm not sure why, but you can believe it. You know how different we are—and I'm more different than you."

He saw a little tremor run over her as she sat gazing at him. Because he was unkillable, he wondered, or because—

"Because I love you," she said, and she kissed him and gave him a shove. He climbed out, stuck his head back in to grin and salute her, then went through the gate while she drove sadly back to Urbanova.

NINETEEN...

Watching the Martian towns drift by beneath her, Harriet cursed her little sportjet's lack of speed. The landscape would have been unrecognizable to the early settlers, but she wasn't interested in either sightseeing or history. To a woman accustomed to high velocities, this was akin to snail-racing.

The handsome woman with the mahogany skin was still trying to understand how she'd missed Harmon with a full clip of needles—when he'd been a clear target. *Harmon.* She still shuddered at the sudden utter panic that had filled her, hurling her forward to merge with the jam of females fleeing the lezbar. There'd been some tough dykes in that crowd, but they'd collapsed into a gaggle of goosey femmes.

I didn't do too well myself. Why'd I run, babbling that sauce about a . . . a garden? Like a hysteric . . . she had cowered in that little hotel for days. Now . . . now a chill of superstitious horror caressed her as she remembered: no one else has been able to shoot Harmon, either. Now he was following her like an avenging superman, and she felt uncomfortable akin to a mindless sheep bleating before him. *How was he doing it?*

She tried to remember if she'd left clues; surely not. The second vizcall might have tipped him to something, but . . . where could he have gone from there? There was no indication of her intent to return to Mars. She—her back-racing mind stopped with a jolt. She frowned. *Where did I go that morning?*

(Roland had entered her room to look at the little package she held. "Going to do some business, partner?"

("Pos. No sense wasting the trip. Make it pay!" She'd thrust the box into her jac pocket. "It'll only take a few minutes to drop this off with a fence."

("Don't take too long, Harriet. We're on a time schedule, and I don't want one deviation. Harmon could be a ruthless competitor."

(She eyed him with poorly concealed distaste. "I've seen some nasty stuff in the rackets, Roland, but this is the topper, deliberately trying to drive a man fobbo by torturing his girl friend!"

(He merely smiled. "Jab away, Harriet, I can absorb any amount of it. I have my reasons . . . and you are being well—very well—paid. You will also have no direct connection with the act."

("Yeah. I'll go along as long's there's money in it. And I'll be back soonest." She stepped out into the hall, closed the door behind her and strode briskly down the . . .

(. . . briskly up the hall and reached for the door. A wave of panic rolled over her. She checked her watch. *One hour and thirty-five minutes.* She touched her pocket. The Star Pearl was gone. Where? Where had she been? Her only memory was of walking out this door!)

Balearic had neither known nor noticed; he was interested only in getting the stones into distribution. She had bluffed her way out of that one. But now, whipping across Mars, she felt that panicky *uncertainty* again. And tried to laugh. No! *I couldn't have given it to Harmon. I'm a little mixed up, but not that bad.*

She watched the flow of the marscape beneath, humming a tune that had died millenia before Ur of the Chaldees crept from the mud of the Euphrates.

Shadows stretched long fingers across the sunset land as her little craft approached the Martian nightside. The lights of Troy appeared, dim through a distant ground haze, and Harriet locked on to the rental agency's beam. The landing was simple and smooth.

Dropping lightly to the ground with her suitcase, she saw the dark form of a man approaching through the dimness. "That you, Mitch?"

"Pos." He trotted over. "Didn't expect you back for several days. Change your plans?"

"They were changed for me," she said, trying to laugh. "Office still open?"

"For about two more mins. You can get your refund if you hurry—otherwise you'll have to wait till morning. New girl; she leaves a few mins early, to catch the cross-town railer."

"Thanks." Harriet lifted her bag—

and climbed into the jet to make his check of the instrument readings

—and strode with long-legged grace to the agency office. The girl was just emerging, and Harriet called to her.

"Uh . . . my railer's almost due . . ."

"I'll drive you wherever you're going," Harriet told her, making a quick evaluation of the girlish face, trying to decide what was under the Martian longcoat. "I'd rather do that than come all the way back in the morning."

"All right." The girl reopened the door. "Come on in, and thanks."

"Thank you," Harriet said, following her in and dropping the bag. She watched the girl flip off her scarf and shake out her hair, automatically arranging a vagrant lock with quick fingers. *Very young,* Harriet thought. *Straight out of the creche.* Curbing her whistle when the girl shrugged off the long striped coat, Harriet pretended to be reading the nameplate on the bulging tunic-top.

"Sylvee," the girl told her, activating her desk. Harriet nodded and waved a hand.

"Harriet," she said. "You're so beautifully breasty I could barely read it."

Sylvee looked up quickly, flushing. "I hear that from men, but not female customers."

"Most females don't acknowledge anything good but themselves," Harriet told her, going to work. The tip of her tongue moistened her lips. "And men . . . they sure can make a compliment sound icky, can't they?"

Sylvee stared, lifting an eyebrow. "So right. Could—could I see your license, please?"

Going to be *easy*, Harriet thought. . . .

. . . and it was, and when she left Sylvee's apt hours later she was superbly relaxed. All that ugliness and fear was drained out of her, and from now on she'd certainly avoid—

. (*for many days she'd moved through the jungle, avoiding other villages, and now she stumbled up the rocky incline. Sharp stones bit viciously at her bare feet, almost unnoticed in her concentration on her goal. Her breath came in ragged gasps, now, as she climbed higher up the narrow path toward the Garden of God. A rock slipped, rolling, and she*)

—cried out in baffled fear, losing her balance to stumble hard against the side of her car. Rebounding, she fell to the ground. She crouched there whimpering in elemental fear, looking about. She was alone. There was no path, no hill, no garden, no god. Rising shakily to her feet, she leaned against the car while she wiped the perspiration from her forehead.

"Am I going buggo? It was so damned REAL!"

She fumbled the car door open and collapsed weakly inside, holding her head in her hands. She could not stop her trembling. *Where did I take that Star Pearl? Why couldn't I hit Harmon with a full clip, and what is the Garden of God?*

She started the car and eased it up only a little, driving carefully. But her head was swimming, writhing inside with unaccustomed sensations; as though she were a musical instrument and someone was plucking her strings to breathe haunting life into melodies long forgotten. She tightened her grip on the steerstick and concentrated on the sparse traffic, and unsought remembrances tempted her psyche into curious bypaths where——

(*she walked in the gardens of Babylon among multiracial throngs that flowed in human tide toward the Euphrates from all corners of the known world, and she was*

165

*aware that she walked alone toward other times: Shalimar,
Peking, the last living human in Machu Picchu watching
the last sunset over the peaks of the Andes as she waited
for oblivion, and wandering in the midst of Golden Gate
Park in San Francisco while the foghorns in the bay
wended their dirge for eternity and the shadows of time
enveloped her mind in the long night of the ever lost)*

—strange roads bent and branched in a silent march
to infinity. A haunted woman brought the car down above
the streets of Troy on Mars, parking with automatic reactions, then walking, unseeing, through the lobby of the
apartment house.

°She's reaching the breaking point, Corland!°

°No cause for alarm. Merely fragmentary genetic re-
tentions. There's no conflict involved, Balearic, and we're
ready to block instantly when she reaches critical cohesion
level. She will have no difficulty surviving this part of it.°

°The Antagonist is accepting it at face value.°

Smug delight. °The Antagonist doesn't believe that we
can exist, much less what we can *do*.°

Harriet closed the door quietly, gazing in confusion
around the suddenly drab apt. She walked over to the
mirror and touched her cheek with two fingers.

"Another face," she whispered, studying it. Another
name and the same endless searching. What woke me
this time? I remember more?"

She stumbled toward the bedroom, desperation in her
movements, her voice plaintive: "*He* should be here!"
But she viewed a silent and empty room before sighing,
wandering over to sink down on the edge of the bed. She
stared at the wall with empty eyes. *Why doesn't he ever
come for me and take me back to the garden?* And she
answered her own mental question: *He can't. He's always
changing. Maybe he doesn't awake, as I do.*

"Why can't I remain submerged? Why can't I sleep
forever?" Her fingers fumbled with her beltbag, opening
it. She took out the gun and raised it, looking into its
dark muzzle. Her fingers tightened on the trigger. Then

166

her eyes rolled up. The weapon slipped from her hand. She sprawled limply across the bed, without a sound.

°Pattern established! The subject is blocked and Prime Maximus proceeds to contact point.°

°Rather close blocking, Balearic. Lorna$_2$ surfaced and integrated more quickly than expected. She came rather uncomfortably close to blowing her brains out, and there was certainly no reason.°

Unconcern from Balearic: °It wouldn't have accomplished anything. She'd only have reincarnated and—°

°Just what we do *not* want her to do while she's holding that pattern, Balearic. She could generate a rather uncommon paradox, purely aside from destructing two years' planning. And we're on far too tight a schedule to allow time to prepare another plan. Lorna$_2$ *must* be ready to perform the moment you've completed diversionary tactics relative to Harmon.°

°I'll feel like a fool, Corland, dashing about those ruins with Harmon chasing me with that neutron gun.°

°Not so foolish when you consider the advantages. You'll have a better chance to cover the Arcturus Four situation—and it will save you the agony of auto-discarnation.°

Resignation: °A reasonable point. You'll have to assume and maintain the block during that period. I'll have to break off completely.°

°We can handle it, Balearic.°

Sunlight filled the room when Harriet awakened. She looked around in fearful confusion before she was able to adjust to her dual personality. Then the pattern congealed. Her mental processes reassembled in rational coherence. *I've got to warn Roland about Harmon! He's—*

But she couldn't quite remember. Swinging her feet to the floor, she clutched her head in both hands. *I have to live out this life the way it is. I can't blame anyone else for what I am.* Stripping, she entered the shower, trying not to think about the rain falling at the beginning of the world (continuum!). She turned her mind to her meeting with Roland Balearic, attacking that mystery once again with new knowledge . . .

They affect some women—strangely. Which is the whole point, of course. But they won't kill anyone. Not in this dimension, anyhow.

"Universe" would be nearer the truth. One of an infinity of universes coexistent with this one, but separate. It is my intention to conquer a universe.

a universe . . .

. . . parts of a life generator of an entire civilization. Of many civilizations, in fact. Through proper reassembly . . . complete dislocation of mental processes . . .

complete dislocation of mental processes.

"I'll be damned if it will," she snapped aloud. She returned to the bedroom to stand with a finger at her chin, deciding on underclothing—

(*and a figure stepped through the door of the castle and she sank to her knees in wonder. It was God, and she recognized*)

"HARMON!" Harriet swayed, clutching at the dresser, staring at her own reflection in horror. "I didn't know it was *he!* We're trying to *kill* each other—I didn't remember everything!"

°Corland! Lorna$_2$ is deviating. Did you catch her evaluations?°

°They appear to be on course, Balearic.°

°But I didn't say a fraction of what she evaluated from our meeting—I didn't even *mention* the other universe.°

°Of course you did, Balearic. Keep in mind that you are a prisoner. An integral part of you is, at least. You're coordinating from your own variant, but the Antagonist is the controlling factor in your Harmon variant. When it assumes control, you become the fragment that you are in that variant. Is that clear?°

°Of course, of course, I'm a . . . "double agent." But—what happened?°

°Coordination. It was necessary to allow the Antagonist to control Balearic. Had that not happened, they'd know we're intercepting them. Now it's perfectly safe to inform you: you were blocked by the continuum.°

!

°The antagonist overestimates its understanding of the human reaction, you see. The information it gave would have persuaded "Harriet" to drop the whole matter. Her personality status would not have it otherwise. It was necessary to block out everything but the money, the material gain. It couldn't be a complete block, because now her composite must have the information to proceed to point Zero.°

°Why haven't you told me that—ignore. Answer is obvious.°

°Of course it is. The pattern is established and proceeding entirely according to schedule. The expected deviation has occurred: L_1 is digressing under the influence of $Harmon_2$. Their present course is the Hidalgo group. You must intercept and isolate.°

°How did that get past Maximus?°

°He knows about it, but he's blocked out. If he deviates from his own structure, the result will be chaos. $Harmon_2$ is absorbing feedback; nothing can be done about that. The pattern similarity is too well defined. He is heading for 944 Hidalgo with no *surface* understanding of the *reason*, but he's rationalizing to simplify your perception. Be mindful that he remains a part of Prime, and is keeping the structure unified. Isolate him.°

°Pattern clarified, Corland. It's obviously impossible for me to evaluate all points in my present situation. After all, this body—°

°If it were a simple task, Maximus could handle it alone, Balearic. Let's continue to hope that L_2 doesn't determine her structure before contact. Does she show any indication of awareness?°

°None whatever. You're starting to coordinate L_3?°

°I am disassembling the primary blocks. L_3 will be monitoring L_2 from this point. There's no indication that the Antagonist is aware of her existence.°

Harriet touched her face in consternation. *What do I*

remember? Do I really remember anything, or am I going out of my mind? (My *mind?*) *What the flaming hell is this thing between Harmon and Balearic?* She began dressing hurriedly. *I'm going to get a payoff from Balearic and get out of this. It's getting too weird for me.* Fully dressed, she glanced at the mirror—and stared. *What did I put on these pants and boots for? I'm not going to space.*

She shrugged her shoulders in wretched resignation. *Okay . . . but I'm fast becoming a case for psyconditioning!* She buckled on belt and pouch and headed for the door. In the doorway she paused to take her keys from the pouch and pocket them, then drop the spare clips for her gun in another pocket, adding even more bulge to her breast. She retained her gun, tossing the pouch back into the room. Then, gun in hand, she stepped out, closing the door—

and put the gun to his head, pulling the trigger in a deafening crescendo of voluntary self-demolition

hurled herself into the path of the oncoming train, her ears dimly reporting the screams of horrified onlookers

°Corland! She's unstabilizing the continuum!°

°DO NOT PANIC. It can't be helped at this point. She's still blocked off, and L$_3$ is taking control. Block out that area. You're feedbacking, and she's picking it up as a diversionary influence. "You" arranged another attempt on her life, remember?°

—and threw herself to the floor of the hall, rolling as she hit the carpet, coming over onto her belly. Her little pistol was spitting hissing fire to slam into the chest of the man at the head of the staircase. He doubled over, his needler drilling futile barbs into the carpet. The man behind him was triggering rapidly as Harriet lurched to her feet and plunged toward him. Needles ricocheted from the walls, singing like angry bees. A flaming, bubbling hole appeared in his forehead, jerking him back to roll down the steps.

Completely unscathed, Harriet raced down the steps. No sense in trying the elevators; someone was waiting downstairs. She knew it. Illogical as the situation was, she no longer doubted. She knew now, beyond any doubt, why it was impossible to kill Wesley Harmon . . . and her.

The soundproofed walls of the apt brought to the battle the semblance of a dream. No doors were flung open; no outcries came from the apts lining the halls. Harriet bounded down four flights without interference. Two men stood at the main entrance. She fired without warning, knowing precisely the nature of their mission. Hands in the act of dying moved toward weapons they could never reach.

She gave the bodies no further thought, merely stepping across them to open the door. She stood still, squinting, probing across Troy.

"That damned Balearic's left the planet!" She loped to her car, took it straight up without regard for the traffic that was almost nonexistent anyhow, and swung toward the spacefield. *I was right the first time. He did hire GunTek to kill me. Well, he won't find safety on Hidalgo—I'll blow his vutting brains out.*

TWENTY...

Noticing the slight deviation on the proximity dial, Randy cut the alarm before it sounded. He activated the viewscreen, let the instruments focus themselves on the object, and increased the magnification. He drew in his breath sharply. The other ship was civilian, close, bigger than his.

He thought he had chosen a route that would keep him and Lorna totally out of contact with other IP traffic. Now—the people on that other ship might have some questions. As fast as his Gambian craft, it was matching his velocity. It was also large enough to contain a crew of several men, as well as a transit tunnel. He watched helplessly as it closed the gap between them, making no attempt at communication.

He had to tell her. "Lorna. Come here."

She appeared in the con cabin entranceway, brushing back a lock of long red hair. Her eyes questioned him, then swerved to the screen.

"Oh, no! Oh Randy, they've *found* us!"

He put his arm around her shoulder and drew her close, squeezing her as comfortingly as he could. "Maybe not. It isn't a League ship. There's no sense in thinking of fleeing or fighting."

They watched the other ship grow larger and larger, filling the viewplate. The noises at the airlock told Randy that it was locking on. Feeling more helpless than a man should ever feel, he waited. The inner lock swung open. Three men entered his ship. All carried guns. The slender man with gray-streaked hair and the flat eyes looked around.

Lorna stared in horror at him, then screamed. She fainted.

The man peered sharply at him. "*Do you know who you are?*"

"Of course I know who I am, schmuck! Who are *you*?"

"Name's Roland Balearic," the man said, tilting his head to study Lorna. "Well," he said softly, "they were actually able to regenerate her without any scar tissue. Excellent! Very well done—but she looks awfully young. And a little plumpish . . . good again." He raised his eyes to Randy, smiling. "Don't hold her so tightly, Randoban Kolumbu. We have no . . . uh . . . designs on her, believe me. You know only your name, eh? That's good, too; anything more would only complicate matters that are already extremely complex."

"What the vut are you talking about, old man?"

Roland laughed. "Believe me, you're better off not knowing. I think it's safe to assume you're creche runaways. Where'd you expect to run to, out here?"

Randy's aggressive attitude slipped seriously. "We're not hurting you, or anyone else. We're just trying to get to Callisto, where there's no discrimination against mating."

"*Callisto.*" Roland stared at him, then waved a hand about the ship. "In *this*? Oh, come now, youngster. This must be the first thing you've ever piloted. It would never make it."

Randy looked chastened. "It has a big enough fuel supply!"

Roland shrugged. "Makes no difference. At the velocity you've been maintaining, your engines are already strained to the bustpoint, bet on it." He looked steadily at the young black man. "They'd blow up before you reached your destination, Randoban." He followed the lie with a quick digression: "But this chatter is useless. You'll find out when she wakes. I used this young woman as a weapon against someone else."

"You!"

"I. If I hadn't, you'd never have met her; think on that one. Now. You have stumbled into the path of an important operation. I'll have to . . . place you in a neutral position. Please offer no objections—we *will* use these guns if we have to."

Looking from Roland to his silent followers—and their guns— Randy sighed. His voice was desultory: "We won't give you any trouble."

Roland nodded and holstered his pistol. "In turn, we'll see you get where you're going. I have no enmity toward either of you, and there's been an inordinate amount of bloodshed already." He stepped back and gestured, rather grandiloquently, at the airlock. "Please come over to my ship. You will be my guests for a while."

Randy started to rise, struggling with the limp girl.

Roland smiled. "I see that the girl is slightly pregnant, if such a thing is possible. The safety of her fetus depends entirely on your discretion and tractability, Kolumbu."

Wesley Harmon studied Roland's features with interest. It was his first view of the man—and it was still impossible to break through the fellow's barrier. Without the availability of the Randoban persona as a vehicle, as eyes, the inspection could never have occurred. It was obvious, from the problems he represented, that Roland Balearic was not a simple entity. Wes watched Randy's gleaming black hands tighten on Lorna's pale flesh as he passed the other men, and smiling, Harmon broke contact.

His fingers made a rapid course adjustment even while he contemplated the ship following him. Probing the area, he found that the pattern was still consistently familiar. He nodded in satisfaction before blanking out the information. Then he reached out toward the orbit of 944 Hidalgo—

checking the readings on the nuclear power plant. Briefly, his mind pictured the layout of the dwelling units as he adjusted the energy output. He left the room, closing and securing the shielded port. He passed through the

174

connecting tube, entered the main dwelling unit, and dropped the little clipboard on the desk.

"All clear, Sam."

Sam yawned, stretching. "Gets monotonous, doesn't it? But the pay's good. Ever wonder where a prospector gets the cred for a layout like this, Marve?"

Marve shrugged. "What's the difference? GunTek doesn't ask questions. Guns and technicians for hire, that's the business. Where the customer gets his cred is his affair —so long's he pays our fee."

"Spoken like a true company man!" Sam laughed. His chair creaked when he leaned forward to toss a message tape to the other man. "Tack this up. Balearic's bringing in a pair of prisoners."

"Prisoners?" Marve studied the tape. "Where'd he get prisoners?"

Sam shrugged. "Couple of creche runaways he picked up off a stolen ship. Wants to hold them until he clears up this operation of his."

"I wonder what the sauce they were doing out here in the boonies," Marve mused aloud. "Why'd anyone run away from a creche? Gov gave us everything, and I never had more sex in my life. I swear, Sam, these kids nowa- days have no sense of responsibility or anything else."

Sam raised an amused eyebrow. "You mean they're not honest businessmen like us, ready to cut a throat for a cred. "Let's not start analyzing young'uns—at least, Balearic hasn't said anything about wanting them deaded. This's been a cozy contract so far. Be a shame to mess up a nice place like this with a lot of blood."

"You're getting too comfortable," Marve grinned. "I think I'll recommend you for a deader contract when we get back."

"Just don't do it till I've had my vacation." Sam rose and headed for the inner door. "I'd better wake up the others. It's time for their watch." He yawned, closing the door behind him.

—and surveyed the silent con cabin of the courier ship. (For the hundredth? thousandth? time) Wes drew out the little box containing the Star Pearl. Opening it, he looked into the depths of the gem with (full knowledge of what it really was, but he still had) no idea of why it had been used. He wondered who he really was—but again something blocked his path to full information.

He stabilized the Harmon pattern . . .

evaluated the impetus of the enemy Antagonist . . .

correlated the potential of Antagonist One . . .

blocked out the Af creche . . .

unified the L_2 composite relay structure . . .

keyed in the Lorna Maximus persona, and . . .

coordinated the continuum.

TWENTY-ONE...

The cargo spacer eased slowly toward the rugged mass of rock that was 944 Hidalgo. Drifting in its fantastic orbit high above the plane of the ecliptic, the asteroid was a lone traveler in eternity. Beyond it, the stars glittered against the ebony backdrop of space. The wan light of the distant sun touched sharp peaks, hurling into the hollows and valleys shadows dark as moonless midnight. Nestled on a comparatively flat area was the white outline of the dwelling units. The ship moved cautiously downward, nosed into one of the docking ports. Magnetic grapples seized the bow and guided it inside.

While Randy and Lorna were hurried away by two armed men, Roland turned to a maintenance crewman. "We won't be here long. This will be the last major haul, and the job will be finished. You haven't touched any of those storage crates, have you?"

Marve shook his head. "Nosir. GunTek is honest, and we abide by contract. By the way, you know you've been followed?"

"My partner, perhaps. She doesn't trust me overmuch."

"Might be, but she can't handle two ships at once. Sensors show two ships, both coming both looking like couriers. One might be your partner—but what about the second?"

Frowning, Rolland shook his head. "I don't know. Stay ready; there's nothing to do until whoever it is gets here."

177

He waved a hand. "Meanwhile get those storage crates loaded onto a jetsled. Careful; they contain some delicate instruments I'll need outside."

Roland brushed past the man and closed the door after him when he entered his office. He relaxed behind the desk with a sigh of relief.

"The matrix is completed," he told the empty room. "It's what you wanted— No, I accept no responsibility for the Harmon situation— Now look, I'm only a fragment. I really don't care one way or the— Now wait a minute! I tried to explain to you what the prisms are. They are *not* generators of life. They are simply identity patterns implanted in energy receptacles; genetic prime patterns. That's *all*—All right, let's forget that; call them generators, if you wish. Is the structure I arranged creating the desired effect in your Universe? . . . Limited chaos— It's your own funeral, since you insist on trying to overthrow something bigger than you."

He toyed with a stylus, apparently listening with infinite patience. Then: "You brought me to the surface when the Balearic pattern dissolved. You were able to do that only because of my pattern's similarity to yours. You're able to control me only because I'm a fragment, and there were several billion of you backtracking the genetic disturbance. It should be obvious to you that your opponents would also be able to do the same, once you had me set up the matrix to unbalance their contin— I *reported* to you that they were alerting the Harmon pattern and using it as a signal output to locate this univer— Of course, you couldn't use me. I am *not* a full pattern, but *Harmon* is— Yes. He is approaching point Zero— Very well. I will be there at breakthrough, and you can fight over the generators to your heart's content . . . assuming you have hearts— No, it's your funeral, not mine. I exist only because you insist on it, Antagonist."

°Did you pick that up in its entirety?°

Affirmation from Corland. °Quite clearly. The Antagonist you're in contact with appears to have greater admiration for its own abilities than the situation warrants.°

178

°Linear continuum. They have only one reference point, so naturally all their "logic" stems from it. They just don't understand the implications to them of that one simple fact: there was only *one* Survivor.°

°The artificially imprinted genetic patterns he carried were real enough, so far as energy content was concerned.°

°No dispute, Corland. He imprinted the patterns on the third-planet aborigines, and intermating made each of them an individual. But the *basic* patterns were still energy, and they formed continua in separate directions, moving toward infinity with each generation. Then he intermated with his sister—°

°The post-aborigine imprinted with his sister's pattern, Balearic.°

°—which set the future in locked lines: the intermating of their descendants created Prime Maximus. The Survivor remains dominant over the entire continuum, but the structure of the continuum itself assures universal reincarnation. That first pattern set it off; an infinite chain-reaction resulting in us: Primes.°

The other Primes and I continue to exist as sentient life whether we reincarnate or not. And the world, the universe, we live in is a dangerous one. °This existence would be more pleasant, Corland, if we could communicate *physically*.°

Wistful enthusiasm. °It would be nice to associate with our own kind, yes. Perhaps in the future; the paradox problem is too great now. We'd not have this problem if the Survivor had mated with the *first* prismated aborigine. But with the continuum separated into infinite variants— what choice have we?°

Amusement. °He couldn't mate with it, it was male. You might as well say we'd have no divergent continuum problem if only energy were not involved. But identity is energy. And so . . . the Antagonists. The prisms left behind. Apparently they had no fully developed patterns. The position of 944 Hidalgo permitted a low-level bleed-through into their universe. I suppose the result was inevitable. The sole purpose of the prisms was to transmit identity. So . . . the Antagonists grab at a chance for *physical* existence, by invading this universe. Using me as their agent.°

°And Prime Maximus had to surface in Harmon's mind, rather remaining normally quiescent. And Harmon had to be . . . helped, to get him to come out and coordinate. I agree: one can't blame the Antagonists. They impressed themselves on self-reproducing entities. Thousands of independent genetic identities, thousands of totally linear continua on a physical level. Nothing in common, no crossovers, no Primes. Hard to visualize that sort of situation; entire genetic lines unable to communicate with each other!°

°But consider our own continuum. They could never grasp its structure, which is why they have no notion that you and I are in communication, or that we're building a trap for their entire system.°

°It is . . . sad. I wish they hadn't bothered us.°

°It isn't so bad, Corland. Think about it: we seldom have the opportunity to converse. Only once every few thousand years.°

°Good point! Speaking of which: point Zero is approaching.°

Rising from the desk, Roland went to the door. "Get the jetsled ready. I'm going outside." He turned to lift out the components of a spacesuit from the locker, fastening the segments to his body with confident motions. He locked the helmet, adjusted the air tanks, tested. Then he headed out to the docking area and the waiting sled.

He climbed in. The inner port closed; air was evacuated from the chamber. The outer port opened smoothly, exposing a view of jagged rock against airless space. With small touches of the firing button, he eased the sled out and floated for a moment above the surface in the almost-complete absence of gravity outside the sealed dwelling unit. With a little smile at the buildings, Roland activated the stern jets. The sled shot out across the desolate wasteland, skimming just above the sharp peaks.

Two thousand miles above the surface, Wes Harmon matched Hidalgo's velocity. His craft seemed to hang motionless in space while he examined the asteroid's rough hulk. He focused on Balearic, pinpointing his location by the peculiar block that made penetration impossible. The man was surrounded by a weird aura of existence/nonexistence that seemed to extend beyond his presence toward . . . an infinite point?

Wes tracked the Balearic aura across fifty miles of the planetoid, until it reached the shallow edge. Then it began moving back around, in the general direction from which it had come. Harmon's fingers moved to the controls. His ship began its approach to Hidalgo. The screen showed him an expanse of low, rolling hills, quite unlike the other, jagged side.

This was a slice of the actual surface of the shattered planet that had given birth to Hidalgo and the other asteroids.

Easing to the surface, Wes let the engines idle for a few moments, then cut them off. Hidalgo's mass was sufficient to hold the ship in place. After suiting up, he wrapped a gauntleted hand around the neutron rifle and moved to the airlock.

He stepped out onto the airless surface of the asteroid . . . and remembered how it had once looked, time out of mind. Home. The green of grass, the songs of varicolored birds beneath a clear blue sky that had shattered into the desolation of cold eternity.

His big shoulders moving in a sigh, he switched on the belt controls. The shoulder rockets lifted him upward.

TWENTY-TWO...

Roland Balearic stood beside the jetsled in a fantastic setting. Surrounding him were ruins that had been preserved for hundreds of thousands of years by the vacuum of space. Shattered buildings raised poignant fingers into the black sky, the agonized gestures of dying giants. Great columns lay on the ground or floated at various levels and unpredictable degrees above the surface. The silence of an eternal graveyard hovered over the scene. The glittering myriads of stars stared down with cosmic disinterest. The silence seemed thick, heavy.

In normal gravity the crates he lifted would have required more strength than he possessed. Here they were featherlight, and he held them on his shoulder as he walked, carefully, toward a sprawling courtyard that had once spread before a splendid structure. In the center of the court, a mechanical device towered into the airless sky: a curious, phallic object, solidly braced on four steel struts. He had spent a year bringing it here, in small, discreetly purchased parts. A piece at a time, it had been assembled to tower above this dark wasteland. The metal of its finished engines glittered with the reflections of the stars.

Lowering the crates to the cracked tiles, he glanced up to the ungainly capsule-like structure atop the mass of

182

metal. He removed a complex of instruments from one crate and activated his shoulder rockets. He drifted lightly upward until he had reached the top of the machine, then braced his feet solidly against the framework. Opening the capsule, he began assembling the instruments within. And returned to open another crate.

After an hour of work, the spacesuited man drifted back to the surface of Hidalgo and surveyed his construction a moment before double-checking the radio-control box at the edge of the courtyard. He smiled, satisfied at last and almost finished.

°It's quite illegal, you know. The Terran League would never permit a civilian to construct such a thing.°

°Our only law, Balearic, is the survival of the continuum.°

°You know, it's rather nice out here. So peaceful, so quiet.°

°Even in your prison?°

°That part isn't pleasant, no. I am talking about the view, Corland, the *feel*. Of course it might well look hideous to those who do not remember it. [He gestured toward the far end of the court.] Remember the old man who used to sell flowers over there at the corner?°

°Oh, yes. I once bought some, for a girl. I often wondered where he lived, where he went at night. A fixture like that raises questions in people's minds. The poor fellow had a devil of a time the first day of the Wind. All of his flowers blew into the pool that was over there at the entrance to the square. Were you here that day?°

°I was. And I have to admit the blossoms made a beautiful sight, floating in the water. The old fellow was quite good-natured about it all. Such a charming personality. You remember people like that. Well. Can you think of any final touches?°

°It would be nice to emblazon it with a fitting inscription—a grossly insulting one. But they"d never be able to read it.°

°I rather think they won't have time to read much of

183

anything, if they read, Corland. They will be too busy wondering what hit them.°

°They will indeed. Balearic, well done. It is a beautiful lithium bomb.°

TWENTY-THREE...

Harmon flew low over the memory-haunted landscape, noting here and there the fragments of things he had once known. He followed a stretch of almost perfectly preserved road that led to the distant ruins of a city slumbering eternally in the black abyss of the cosmos. At a crossroads, he gazed at the blasted ruins of what had been a delicate temple structure—(*playing on the steps in the warm light of spring when he was very young . . . the fragrance of new-rising grass . . . the perfumes of the garden . . . the two young girls who*) seemed to drift beside him on this errand of destruction. Grimly he returned his attention to the distant city.

Approaching the desolate metropolis, he cut the power of his jets and directed himself groundward. The dust of eternity drifted up around him in a slow cloud when his booted feet touched. He stepped forward, leaving the dust cloud to its fate. He moved into the ruins. Rounding a fallen colonnade, he stared across the broad avenue, lined with crumbled structures and nearly choked with scattered debris. So silent! The road stretched into the distant wreckage. He walked along the ancient road, passing scattered and mainly demolished vehicles. He marveled at one that remained almost intact save for its pitting with the scars of cosmic pebbles, god's garbage, that periodically pelted the asteroid.

He detected Balearic in the city and altered his course

toward a seemingly impassable mass of ruin. The shoulder rockets carried him over and he managed an almost-graceful landing. Moving cautiously through the eternal shadows, he at last saw the spacesuited figure standing in the distant wreckage. He moved steadily closer. There was no longer any question about the identity of that solitary man amid ghostly silence.

The voice came in his helmet com: "Hello, Harmon."

Wes was silent for a moment. Then, "You're a dead man, Balearic."

Balearic chuckled. "What makes you so sure I ever lived?"

"You were alive enough to torture Lorna," Wes said, tightening his grip on the neutron rifle until his fingers hurt, "and you're alive enough to die. I wish I could tie you up and go over you with a hot iron, slowly."

"A lot of things are going to die, Harmon. But my time is not quite yet."

"Your time is right now!" Whipping the rifle to his shoulder, Wes tightened his finger on the trigger—

—and stared in consternation.

Balearic had vanished.

"Your reflexes are too slow, Harmon!"

Wes spun and fired at the figure behind him.

Balearic vanished.

"Your reflexes are too slow, Harmon!"

Wes spun again. Balearic stood nonchalantly on the apex of a tall column. Glowering, Wes lowered the rifle. "Cute. Teleportation?"

"Well, that's oversimplifying . . . it's a good catch-all phrase covering a multitude of complicated factors. Time, space, genetics." Balearic smiled. "Of course, it's all within the rules of this universe."

"Didn't look that way to me," Harmon said. "How'd you do it?"

Balearic shrugged. "You already know what I did, and how."

186

"What's the game, Balearic? You think I came out here to play riddley-riddley-ree?"

Balearic chuckled. "Of course not! You came out here to kill me. You have to, eventually, but I notice you've resigned yourself to the fact that it can't be done until *I* am ready. I can displace myself faster that you can pull that trigger."

"I admit I can't shoot a man who can do what you just did," Harmon said, not without exasperated anger. "But you still haven't answered my question. How'd you change position so fast?"

"Don't worry about killing me," Balearic said equably. "You can do it. I speak from first-hand experience . . . I was there when you did it. But never mind about that now. We'll get to it in good time. As to my moving so fast . . . well I didn't move at all. I've been to Acturus Four."

Harmon sighed. "Oh, come on, Balearic. You can't travel to a star, change your position on this asteroid, and still remain in one place. The statement contradicts itself."

"No, no. On the contrary. The time factor in this instance is a variable, so the space factor is also a variable." Balearic laughed, briefly. "They are really the same thing seen from different points of view, but we have to separate them to pretend to understand them. Or understand *it*. Distance is only the movement of an object through time. If you prefer looking at the other side of the coin, time is only the distance involved in the movement of an object. Do you grasp the idea?"

"Naturally. I'm not dense."

"No," Balearic said quietly, "you most certainly aren't. I know what you are. It should be obvious that the *object itself* is the time-space factor."

"And the object generates its own environment."

"Obviously everything I've said is quite possible. The space-time continuum of the Antagonists is vastly different. A minute here is centuries there. It's only a relative consideration, but real, nevertheless. I am trapped by the continuum of the Antagonist—but I am related to the spacetime matrix of *this continuum*. By using *their*

187

matrix in relation to this one, it's possible to reorient all of it. As a result, I did not move. I was there and now I am here. I know you can kill me, because you already have. Is that clear?"

"Clear as a magician's patter," Wes said. He cradled the rifle in the crook of his arm. "So you violated the laws of mass and velocity."

Balearic shrugged. "Laws are credible only when they're obeyed, and it wasn't necessary for me to obey the laws you mentioned. Of course, this is merely repetition; after all, *you* told me how to do it."

"Are you crediting me with super powers?"

"*Do you know who you are?*"

Instantly Wes did. "I am Prime Maximus."

The man atop the fluted pillar saluted him jauntily.°Of course you are. And no, you have no more power than any other human, under ordinary circumstances. But these circumstances are far from ordinary. Your power is what and who you are. You are master of your domain: the entire genetic continuum. I suppose that might be called super power, from an analytic point of view. Maximus: you have the Star Pearl?°

Wes slapped one of the belt-pouches of his spacesuit. °Of course. But it's only a pattern.°

°Ex-cellent,° Balearic smiled. °You are eliminating the blocks in perfect order. Hold onto the pattern. You must install it yourself.°

°I assume the bomb is ready,° Maximus said, glancing up at the distortions in the sky.

°Fully assembled. I installed the lithium warhead just before you arrived. You won't have an easy time getting to it, though.°

Maximus shrugged. °Of course not, but I will complete the cycle. After all, we fought this war two years ago.°

°That was feedback, Maximus. This is the real thing. You must go through the entire course of events. You have no choice—it has already happened. We won, because of the distortion of the time factor. That, combined with their linear genetic continuum, demolished them in the beginning.°

°It was rather a hopeless conflict,° Maximus agreed. °It should never have been started. Which is a useless statement. There was no way to stop myself from starting it.°

°Obviously. Roland Balearic is you,° Balearic stated. °A perfectly stable variation of the Prime pattern you created by mating with the reincarnation of your sister. You returned here to 944-H because you know what it is. Your subconscious has held all the information always. You found these ruins because you know where to look. All that would have been perfectly safe if you hadn't found the genetic patterns. That was what blew everything sky-high.°

°Fate,° Maximus suggested.

°It's as good a word as any, Maximus. We are not, after all, gods. But—°

°Oh, *I* was, once.°

Balearic chose to ignore: °But non-Primes would think so, if they knew we existed. Gods . . . or devils.°

°They must know we exist. They talk too much of ghosts, and certainly we look that way on occasion. They also talk of telepathy, which is nothing but recognition of the genetic continuum. If they caught any of us, they'd probably burn us at the stake.°

°They have. A useless animal gesture; we merely reincarnated. They do the same thing themselves, on a lesser level. But they refuse to believe even that. All to the good . . . that way they don't interfere with the coordination of the Variant Primes.°

°They do make complications, though. Everything I did had to look normal. I had to arrange for poor Lorna to be regenerated to an earlier age, so her memories would not fade naturally. Obviously I couldn't *kill* her; I love her too much. But the Antagonists thought the torture would break my Harmon mind so that I wouldn't interfere. It worked into the plan perfectly. It provided . . . cover. I'm sorry you had to be involved in that. It must have hurt.°

Balearic, like a moving statue atop his pinnacle, shrugged. The conversation continued, in utter silence. °It couldn't be helped. We knew from the beginning that would happen. We couldn't break the chain of events. The temporal dislocation showed that they were the only things that could have happened. When the opposing Antagonist determined the correct pattern that would deflect the attack on your mind, we had already constructed L_2 as a conveyor—and a weapon.°

°They're welcome to their generators, as they call them,° Maximus shot back. °We'll see that they collect them all. And they will get one hell of a shock when they find what that means! We can*not* take a chance on this sort of thing happening ever again.°

It began.

The sky commenced twisting in on itself. The stars were as viewed through a distortion lens. A vortex of rippling, shuddering light flashed across the ruins, bathing it in madhouse splendor. °They're coming through, Balearic? I'll have to destroy that pattern the moment they relax control of it—its coherence is demolished anyhow. Good-bye, Balearic!°

The figure atop the colonnade jerked as though struck with an electric shock. It toppled to the ground, screaming, arms and legs flailing wildly. The screams told Maximus that Balearic had devolved, back into the main pattern. The man-figure touched the ground and scrambled in a mad flight across the tumbled ruins. Raising the neutron rifle, Maximus pressed the trigger, and a ravening stream of energy flashed toward the fleeing madman. He felt a moment of hideous pain as the bolt disintegrated his nuclear pattern.

Then he regained his stability and knew that he was dead.

Incandescent distortion swept across the sky. They whirled in a great vortex above the ruins, illuminating them in radiant lunacy and twisting the shadow of Maximus into patterns of delirium. Incarnadine mists billowed amid the ghost-silent ruins. Maximus activated his shoulder jets and rushed toward the bomb. Microseconds crept by like individual eternities while diabolic shadow shapes commenced forming at the center of the vortex.

190

The completely alien identity patterns made it impossible to determine the nature of the conflict in progress.

And then the vortex spilled incredible monstrosities onto the terrain of Hidalgo. The vanguard of the genetic horrors writhed insanely among the crumbled buildings and debris. Tentacles twisted from unrecognizable body forms. Multiple heads and eyestalks bobbed and twisted. Iridescent beams thrust into space in a web of fantastic force, seeking to reunite the generator. The invasion from the other universe had begun.

TWENTY-FOUR...

"That," Blake of Protectors said, "is all we have to remind us of Wesley Harmon." He indicated the scintillant objects on the desk. "Star Pearls. They affect the minds of the women who wear them—and we do *not* know what they are. They resulted in the unbelievable mutilation of one of Harmon's jays, and the poor guy went completely buggo."

The members of the Procurers Guild board studied the gems with curious—and respectful—eyes. The chairman glanced up at Blake. "And the girl?"

Blake examined his black cigar. "Regeneration and regression. Psychologically and physiologically, she came out of it a teen-aged girl. The police lodged her in an Afro creche before we could get together some Sponsor papers, and she and a boy—well, man—named Randoban Kolumbu took off in a Gambian spacer with the help of his sister. Under drugs, she admitted they were Callisto-bound."

"Wow, *that's* a story," the hyper-jowled man said. "And what about Harmon?"

Blake sighed. "Last time I saw him, he told me to consider him dead if he wasn't back in six months. There's been no trace of him, not even on Mars. It's getting close to a year since he left. Too damned bad; he was a good man and a good pimp."

The board chairman scanned the documents before him.

"The replacement is working out, and the girls have apparently had no trouble in adjusting to him. That right, Blake?"

Blake wiped the cigar out of his mouth. "That's the only good thing to come out of any of it. Paul Mitsubishi clicked perfectly, and the business is in fine shape. A very good man."

The chairman nodded. "I see. And your investigators have made the effort, without finding a trace of either Harmon or the girl?"

"Well . . . She's en route to Callisto—try getting her back from *there!* And Harmon left for Mars, we *think.* Now *that's* all, yes."

The chairman blew out his cheeks. "Gentlemen? Are there any more questions, or should we consider the evidence sufficient?" He waited, then rapped his knuckles on the gleaming desktop. "Done, then. Our legal staff will forward the necessary papers to Mitsubishi confirming his possession of the business vacated by Wesley Harmon. Harmon's personal accounts will be absor—"

Maximus, seeking to make headway toward his destination, twisted through an impossible sea of alien forms—

(*Raising the rifle, Maximus pressed the trigger and a ravening stream of energy flashed out toward the fleeing madman*)

(*raced up the aisle of the planetarium as the guards dived for cover*)

—and switched on shoulder jetpack to leave the road and move up into the ruins. A tentacle writhed toward him, curling around his body—

(*crossed the bridge to the kneeling girl who, even with her downy fur, so resembled his sister*)

—rushed down the wreckage-strewn road into the tumbled ruins. He stayed close to the bases of the buildings to avoid the searching tentacles as the second vortex erupted into existence and disgorged an incredible stream of abominations that closed in a maelstrom of conflict with the first contingent—

(*caught the impression and whirled to look behind him.*

193

Balearic stood nonchalantly on the apex of a tall colon-nade)

Harriet adjusted the direction of her little ship—and knew what was happening. She knew, now her role in this fantastic conflict.

Her fingers moved automatically, grimly increasing velocity toward Hidalgo. The hellishly torn landscape reflected the couriership's passing with brimstone flashes as the jets cast their radiance over shattered rock. Harriet sensed the increasing pressure on the genetic and space-time continua; the Antagonist raced through the barrier of the universe-matrix. The extensions from the other pattern, numbering in the billions, were no more a single entity than . . . she. In the distance, she saw the titanic distortions of the inter-universe conflict. It raged over the ruins in a display of tortured, demonic energy.

Her craft soared over the sharp edge of Hidalgo and curved gracefully into a flat trajectory with the city as its goal. The ponderous ruins rushed toward her. Then she was arcing above the tumbled masonry, and she could see, clearly, the entities from elsewhere. The writh-ing, tentacular vision brought a wave of nausea.

He was diverting them, for her. Now she must divert them, for *Him*.

Her ship leaped high above the city, then plunged downward. It flattened in a fiery path through the can-yons between once-great buildings. The keel jets poured roiling fire and energy down into the embattled hordes that seethed below, a nightmare ocean. Like a hellish scythe of flame, the couriercraft swept across the sub-ancient city. Bolts of unfamiliair energy leaped up to stab at it, but failed to halt its lightning flight.

Maximus noted the ship's passage; it had entered the scene right on schedule, to break, temporarily, the space-time distortion holding him from his goal. He poured power into his shoulder pack, streaking perilously through the towering ruins. Through a network of columns and blasted structures he saw it: the courtyard. The

194

gleaming device that awaited his final adjustments. A mote in the immensity of that desolate arena of death, he rushed upward and clung to the missile's top.

The compartment remained open as Balearic-persona had left it. Maximus worked swiftly, fastening the Star Pearl into its waiting niche, making the delicate connections. Then he swung the panel shut and secured the locking lugs. Drifting away from the towering bulk of deadly machinery, he turned again toward the ground. Once he had himself aimed at the courtyard's edge, he switched on the jets.

His boots touched ground near the little electronic console. His hands went swiftly to the controls.

The complicated open structure of the engine shuddered as power began building in the network of mechanisms, directed by signals from the console. The mouths of the power jets began to glow. Little tongues of flame lapped at the pavement. They extended, burning hungrily at the ancient tiles. Energy poured forth in torrents until a pool of flame churned beneath the missile. It trembled in the throes of its own awakening. The struts quivered, began to lift. The huge machine edged skyward on a pillar of blinding light.

Rapidly increasing its velocity, the hell-missile leaped upward and flashed toward the area of inter-universe combat.

Beams of ravening energy lanced at it as it arced toward the twisting funnel of a vortex that seemed to extend to infinity. Into the diabolic mass of tormented spatial conformations it drove, hammering an irresistible path. Its column of flame became invisible in the incredible radiance of the vortex. It plunged in.

Maximum abandoned the console. The missile was out of contact, no longer within his control, and he was far from finished.

Somewhere in the depths of the space-time continuum, the lithium bomb detonated.

Harriet screamed.

The control cabin of her ship blazed with sudden uncanny luminescence and *she* was there, her crimson gown reflecting the hellish fires of planetary destruction that spread to the horizon behind her. The figure wavered, drifting toward Harriet, emanating wretched confusion.

Harriet staggered from the con. Sweat streamed from her as she watched the apparition speeding nearer. She knew she faced impending destruction/liberation. Whimpering, she sank to her knees. Their patterns meshed. The other realized what was happening, and she strove to break off contact. But both of them were impelled and compelled by a totally irresistible force.

Unseen currents of overload rippled through the genetic continuum as a point of crisis approached, too rapidly.

"I don't want to die/*at last! freedom from this body*," Harriet whispered/thought, but she knew she was already dying, the other pattern merging with her own and channeling her into the continuum. "I don't want to

The ship swerved wildly and plummeted into the raging mass of the Antagonists.

°Free at last!°

"Gentleman, are there more questions, or should we consider the evidence sufficient?" The chairman waited, shrugged, rapped his knuckles on the gleaming desktop. "Done, then. Our legal staff will forward the necessary papers to Mitsubishi confirming his possession of the business vacated by Wesley Harmon. Harmon's personal accounts will be absor—"

He threw his hands before his face and nearly went over backward in his chair; a blinding light filled the room. The air above the Star Pearls on the desk distorted, writhed, curved maddeningly in upon itself in a brain-wrenching distortion of time and space. It was over in a fraction of a second. By the time the occupants of the room could once more focus their contracted eyes on the surface of the desk, it was empty.

The Star Pearls were gone.

Blake took a shaky pull at his cigar. "That's the kind of stuff poor Harmon was involved with," he murmured. "God, he's gone!"

196

And somewhere, in another space-time continuum, several billion entities plunged into the dark abyss of unconditional insanity.

TWENTY-FIVE...

Streaming sweat within his spacesuit, Maximus staggered: the concussion from the lithium bomb wrapped back from infinity to wreak havoc over the zone of conflict. Temporal components twisted into insane
disorder as combatants fought and refought the
    same instant
disorder as combatants fought and refought
    the same
disorder as combatants fought and re
disorder as

A mote within the holocaustic inferno, Maximus gave his shoulder jets all power. Gradually he forced himself out of the temporal turmoil on streamers of flame, soaring across the ruined city toward the wasteland beyond. The monumental struggle slipped rapidly away behind him. In the distance, he sighted the metallic gleam of his ship, renamed MANUEL'S DREAM.

He rushed inside, slapping at air and lock controls, dragging away his suit even as he ran to the con cabin.

Up from the dead landscape he rose, away from the nightmare battleground. It circumnavigated Hidalgo until it again hurtled across jagged peaks and ebon valleys toward the dwelling units. He brought it in, berthed it, locked it. The tunnel rumbled out, connecting his airlock with artificial atmosphere.

He knew what he'd find outside. The temporal disorien-

198

tation was snaking out to this area, now, and the maintenance crewmen were losing their mental hold on reality. He opened the lock. Crazed men swarmed toward him. Needles hummed and sang about him.

The gun bucked in his hand, spouting flame toward the nearest attacker, who stared wildly at the man in the airlock, feeling the burning impact of the .45 caliber bullet as he died . . .

. . . fired a wild shot and died . . . jerked the rifle trigger rapidly and died with a bullet in his head . . . threw down his gun and ran screaming until the killing bullet slammed into his back . . . fired and died and fired and died and/

Tears of pain streamed from Maximus's eyes as he staggered from the airlock. He had felt every one of the bullets, though each had struck only fragmentary incarnations of himself. He swayed drunkenly across the docking area, stumbling over corpses as he fought his way through billowing clouds of smoke. The electrical wiring was beginning to burn, overloaded. Soon, he knew, the radiations from the intercosmic battle would detonate the nuclear reactor.

There was no way to contact the genetic continuum through the space-time turmoil that raged over the asteroid. He could only hope that Randoban and Lorna, Lorna$_1$ and Harmon$_2$, had been kept blocked off. He found the temporary prison, smashed the locks hurled it open to gaze at the naked youngsters within. Catching his breath, Maximus asked sharply, *"Do you know who you are?"*

Randy looked puzzled. "Of course. I'm Randoban Kolumbu."

Good; obviously the young man had no knowledge of the fact that he was a Maximus pattern, that he had/ would play an important part in this monumental conflict. The blocking had been good. Turning to the pale girl clinging fearfully to the black's arm, Maximus asked, quietly:

"Do you know Wesley Harmon?"

"No! *No!*" She pressed her cheek against the boy's chest. "Oh, RANDY! Please take me away from here!"

Maximus sighed, satisfied and delighted. Her memories were gone. The pattern was complete.

He looked back at Randoban. "*You* know who Wesley Harmon is—I'm he. Never tell her. Just get her out of here. This asteroid is about to become a nuclear bomb."

They followed him. Randy stared about the corpse-strewn room as Maximus waved a hand at Balearic's ship. "What happened? Who are these people, Harmon?"

"This ship is your ticket to Callisto. Take it and GET OUT OF HERE!"

Randy leaped into the airlock, spun to drag Lorna up after him, and for a brief moment his eyes met those of Prime Maximus. Then his hand swung to one side and the airlock began to close. The shielded safety panel slid shut. Maximus heard the muted thunder a few minutes later, as the ship roared out of the tube and into deep space.

He was Randoban setting course—

—he was Maximus, smiling with the knowledge that neither Randoban nor Lorna possessed. He knew they were carrying an unexpected passenger.

Insidious needles began prickling at his skin, telling him that the reactor was reaching critical stage. He raced across the big room to the lock of his own ship. Inside, panting, he stabbed a finger at a button and wrenched over a lever. The lock pivoted shut with tantalizing slowness. As soon as it was secured, he rushed to the con cabin and strapped himself in. His hands danced over the console. The ship hurtled out of the tube, streaking across the bleak landscape at tremendous accelerating velocity.

Suddenly the vessel shook and staggered as though slapped by a giant. Maximus knew the reactor had detonated. The seatbelts failed to hold, and his head struck a projection, and darkness gloved his numbed brain.

TWENTY-SIX...

Bells.

Echoes in the stunned cells of his mind.

That vacant place of peace, disturbed by beckoning melodies, recoiled from consciousness, coiling about itself in a quest for continued tranquillity. Then the urgently summoning carillons drew him, dragged him like a magnet. His eyes opened. He stared blankly at the instrument panel.

Abruptly his awakened brain recognized the insistent alarm generated by overstrained engines. Instinctive reactions drove his hands into action. They moved in swift patterns across the board. Flames faded. The tubes still glowed with heat, but now the ship hurtled on with all of the mighty power built from long continuous acceleration. The bow tubes burst into life, and a hell of energy poured from them. For tens of thousands of miles, the ship flamed like a raging comet. A hundred thousand. Two hundred thousand miles. The sweating man kept his eyes fastened on the velocity gradations while his fingers worked automatically at familiar adjustments. The throb of the engines decreased. The couriership and Maximus drifted free in the immensity of space. He sagged back into the seat.

After readjusting controls and setting a medium-velocity course for Mars, he keyed in Auto and again sagged back. His eyes rolled about at the quiet cabin. Silence; it's beautiful. Then he grinned and addressed the empty air.

°Are you there, Balearic?°

°Yes, darling, free at last. And stop calling me that! Two years of it was way too much. What a hell of a body for a girl to be trapped in!°

Maximus laughed. °All right, Lorna Hayakawa. But that's your reward for being a fragment of this variant. This is a dangerous place.°

°Oh, thanks.°

°Did Lorna Maximus implant Harriet successfully? I was entirely too busy to watch.°

°Oh, yes. That was no trouble at all. Lorna and Randoban will give birth to her on Callisto. Coordinator Corland suppressed the false emphasis on her fragments, but not much can be done about the actual memory impressions. They may surface sometime, but she'll probably attribute them to imagination. Of course, if she ever realized what we did to her . . .°

°She'll be a very pissed-off kid.°

Soft laughter. °But not half so pissed off as the Antagonists will be. If any of them survived.°

Maximus nodded. °I'm afraid not. They realized their mistake too late. They thought *Harriet* was the real Lorna, and that they had her helpless. Their linear understanding couldn't let them believe we could make a composite Lorna, out of fragments, and implant them on another identity.°

°Rather bad for Harriet.°

°Um. It left her a perfect channel for the feedback of our sister's pattern, when the bomb went off. Those patterns were too completely sealed by space/time factors; that was the only way we could break them. And what a load of information we gleaned! Think of the rash of inspired inventions that'll be cropping up in our continuum in the next couple of centuries! It will be the biggest breakthrough since Abraham Darby₁ and Darby₂ caught about a minute and a half of feedthrough in the eighteenth century. The Antagonists may have been monstrous, but they certainly understood energy.°

202

°That was fine timing, Maximus.°

°It took all the Variants to do it. The Antagonists' big error was in thinking they were entering one universe. Because of the genetic continuum, ours is an infinity of universes. The Antagonists entered them all, simultaneously. They fell apart, trying to zero in on an infinite number of Prime Variants, all trying to launch an infinite number of lithium bombs. I doubt that they all went off. A lot of them were probably nullified by the time-warp.°

°Surely they weren't all needed . . .?°

°No. I think it's a safe supposition that a large chunk of their universe is a total wreck. That explosion must have raised absolute hell with some of their galaxies. But it isn't a total loss, of course. Enough of those identity units must have been projected to start a few thousand new genetic chains. Let's just hope they don't recrudesce any more self-producing entities. We've seen the ghastly effect of one-track minds.°

°Really, darling, I/Balearic did my best to convince them that our kind of continuum could exist. They just wouldn't believe it.°

°I know. Their whole existence was the result of energy projection, rather than implantation. If there are any left, they've been reduced to idiot level. Anyhow, you're a complete woman again, and you won't have to go through being part of a man. I prefer your own sexy self.°

°I'm glad you love me so much.°

°I love you no matter which Variant you're in, but try to avoid writing your old name in the Old Words, all right?°

Smilingly absorbing her chastened emanations, Wes stood and stretched. He began unbuttoning his shirt. °Care to join me in a shower?°

°I'll pass this time, darling.°

°Nothing to stop you from coming over now, you know.°

°Yes there is, luv. I'm too tired to get myself drilled in a spaceship shower. I think I'll just block out and play normal human.°

Maximus laughed. "All right," he said aloud. "I think

we're all a little worn out. Oh . . . what did you find on Acturus Four?"

Merriment. °A telepathic civilization. Good night, darling.°

Lorna Hayakawa vanished from his perception. He stripped, heading for the showertank. Inside, he contacted the Prime Variant:

°Lorna Maximus. Why so quiet?°

°I am not quiet,° Tommy replied. °I am seething.°

°Now what did I do?°

°I heard you murmuring sweet somethings to my variant.°

°Precisely the same as talking with you, Tommy love.°

°Hardly. When you have something to say to me, don't bother with substitutes.°

°All right, all right, if you want it that way. Care to join me in a shower?°

°*No!* I'm tending bar right now. Imagine the effect on these non-Primes if I suddenly vanished!°

°That's an easy one. They'd believe in witches and warlocks—or re-form Alcoholics Anonymous.°

°It's too early for any of that. I want to hold onto this bar until we figure out our direction. We've got a new thing going, old love, and it's going to take a little thought.°

°Now there's a double meaning, if I ever heard one! I think it would be wise to block out, submerge, so we won't have to face two problems at once. Let them handle it; let Wesley Harmon and Tommy take over again. Until next time.°

°Until next time, darling.°

V: BEGINNING: AGAIN

The sun was setting when Wes Harmon stepped from the ship and took a deep breath of the "fresh" air of Mars. He glanced up at the sky, feeling the peace of a great load's having been lifted from his mental shoulders. Somewhere on a rock in the distant cosmos was the body of the men he had hunted. Nearby was the wreckage of the ship piloted by his (semi)female partner. It was all over. He wondered about Lorna; he hoped she was wonderful.

What remained was to begin a new life. With Tommy— unless something had happened. Months had passed since he had left her. But they had what they had; more than any other couple, anywhere, they had . . . something in common.

He walked down the silent road to Wildcat Row, whose lights were just beginning to glow. In the distance, the spires of Urbanova stretched for the stars, beckoning him like a home beacon. *Home*, he thought. Yes. Earth was the past; Mars and Tommy were forever.

He'd hardly set foot into the little town before the cabbie called. "Looking for a spot of fun, jacko?"

Wes nodded, grinning, and climbed in. He gave the address.

"Uh . . . you new, jacko? Sure that's the right address? Man, that's a lezbar!"

"Right."

Forty minutes later, Wes paid the man—who was still shaking his head—and stepped onto the strange sidewalk. He'd have to accustom himself to its immobility. He glanced up at the narrow entranceway flanked by slim panels of extruglas bricks. The sign was off. He saw no light inside. He pressed close, peering through the little window into the darkened lounge, grinning as he recalled, graphically, what he'd done to Tommy that day he'd met her. Made for each other. *Almost as if I were sent here to find her. Thanks, Harriet and Balearic.*

Wes!

A light appeared at the far end of the room as a door opened. A figure blocked off the light momentarily before hurrying down through the empty chairs and tables. The lock clicked, the door swung open, and he grinned at Tommy, wearing about two ounces of robe and an enormous smile.

Get in here!

He stepped in. She slammed the door, locked it, and buttoned the window into opacity. Then she was throwing

205

her arms around his neck, pressing close, trying to climb his body.

"Oh, darling! I *missed* you so much!"

Wes caressed her through the frivolous robe as she parted her lips for his kiss. She was trembling with eagerness and he pulled her robe apart to smooth his hands over the brown nakedness within. She drew her arms away, just long enough to shrug the robe from her shoulders. It whispered to the floor. She curled her arms around his neck and slapped her bare body against him. He pressed her close.

"I don't mind the floor, Wes . . ."

"I do! In we go." And he carried her through the bar, and minutes later her legs were twined around his waist. And a few minutes after that, they were covered with sweat, gasping and making throaty sounds.

He watched her go to build him a drink. The little green light she waved on cast romantic illumination over the brown body he loved.

"That looks nice," he said, and chuckled as she wagged her hips with wicked exaggeration. He watched, smiling while she mixed two drinks and brought them back to the bed.

"I *hope* it looks nice," Tommy said. "You're going to see an awful lot of it in years to come. I hope you never get tired of looking at it."

He patted her hip. "No way," he said. "No way. There are only two of us, but . . . consider what we have to share. No two people ever had so much."

"I spent so many lonely years," she said, staring at the wall. "You know what I went through. I thought I must be the only one. I was an outsider, everywhere. Always. I knew what everyone else was thinking, but I couldn't admit it, and no one knew what *I* was thinking . . . or cared. Men . . . I . . . they just . . ."

She shivered as he stroked her, gently, wondering how it was that two telepaths suddenly emerged—and of opposite sexes. He wondered. Were other powers possible?

"So I turned to other women," she was saying. "At least they knew how girls think, and what I needed."

Wes let a long trickle of the Martian whiskey slide easily down his throat. He squeezed her breast.

"*I* know what you think, darling. You won't ever have to worry about that again. Now there are *two* telepaths, and we're together, and we can do what *no*body can do."

Knowing each other's thoughts as they whisked out through the continuum and fed back to the two—submerged—halves of Prime Maximus, they leaned forward to kiss. She chuckled, their thoughts of super-people mingling. *You should have been here last night, Wes.*

Too right. And the night before that, and the one before that—

No, no, darling, there was a teleplay I've thought about ever since. One of those super-race things. Do . . . Wes? Do you think we'll start some sort of super-race?

Let's, he thought back. *Who can stop us?* He laughed.

Deep in both their subconsciouses, another kind of laughter rose—but not quite to the surface.

GREAT SCIENCE FICTION FROM WARNER PAPERBACK LIBRARY!

THE FRANKENSTEIN FACTORY   (76-861, $1.25)
by Edward D. Hoch
Yesterday's horror story becomes tomorrow's reality as a team of doctors creates a new man from parts of dead men cryogenically frozen years before.

THE DRACULA TAPE   (78-869, $1.50)
by Fred Saberhagen
With an attention to the details of the original Dracula story, and an amazing knowledge of historical and literary Vampirana, Saberhagen writes this fang-in-cheek adventure in a style that will delight vampire fans and others.

WHEN WORLDS COLLIDE   (76-881, $1.25)
by Philip Wylie & Edwin Balmer
Two outlaw plants are going to collide with Earth! Scientists begin to build rockets to evacuate "the chosen few" to a distant planet to start anew—but word gets out. Mass hysteria brings out the worst, as people fight for survival.

AFTER WORLDS COLLIDE   (76-873, $1.25)
by Philip Wylie & Edwin Balmer
The classic sequel to **When Worlds Collide.** When a group of survivors landed on Bronson Beta they expected absolute desolation. Instead they found a beautiful city—and also found that they were not alone.

 A Warner Communications Company

Please send me the books I have checked.

Enclose check or money order only, no cash please. Plus 25¢ per copy to cover postage and handling. N.Y. State residents add applicable sales tax.

Please allow 2 weeks for delivery.

WARNER PAPERBACK LIBRARY
P.O. Box 690
New York, N.Y. 10019

Name ....

Address ....

City .... State .... Zip ....

_____ Please send me your free mail order catalog